Iris Hanika, born in Würzburg in 1962, has lived in Berlin since 1979. She received the prestigious Hans Fallada Prize in 2006. Her novel *Treffen sich zwei* was shortlisted for the German Book Prize in 2008. *The Bureau of Past Management* was awarded the European Union Prize for Literature and the LiteraTour Nord Prize. She was a resident at the Villa Massimo in Rome in 2017/18. Her most recent novel *Echos Kammern* won the Hermann Hesse Literature Prize in 2020.

Abigail Wender is a poet and translator. Her debut poetry collection, *Reliquary*, was published in 2021. She lives in New York City.

THE BUREAU
OF PAST MANAGEMENT

Iris Hanika

Translated by Abigail Wender

 **Creative Europe**

Co-funded by the Creative Europe
programme of the European Union

V&Q Books, Berlin 2021
An imprint of Verlag Voland & Quist GmbH
First published in the German language as *Das Eigentliche* by Iris Hanika

English edition through Nabu International Literary Agency;
www.nabu.agency

Editing: Katy Derbyshire
Copy editing: Angela Hirons
Cover photo: Unsplash
Cover design: Pingundpong*Gestaltungsbüro
Typesetting: Fred Uhde
Printing and binding: PBtisk, Příbram, Czech Republic

ISBN: 978-3-86391-307-6

www.vq-books.eu

We are ugly, but we have the music.
Leonard Cohen,
'Chelsea Hotel #2'

THERE COMES A TIME when it all falls away – the anger of youth, the sorrow you felt at the world's injustice, and also the confidence that things would get better, maybe even good if you just tried hard enough, put your whole heart into it. There comes a time when that heart empties abruptly and you eddy down into yourself, entirely alone. Not a great time.

SOMETIMES HE RECALLED how he'd always think about the trains headed to concentration and death camps whenever he was on a crowded U-Bahn; how those trains had been even more crowded than the one he was in, and about the absence of any seats in those cattle cars. Graziela had described a scene from the American film *The Pawnbroker* (1964, director: Sidney Lumet) in which there was a leap from the quotidian into the past, and had made the comparison between today's underground trains and the trains to Auschwitz. She said she couldn't get the scene out of her head. At the same time, she continued, it made her feel disgusted with herself for two reasons. For one, it was pretentious of her to compare her dignified and privileged life with those who'd been abandoned by civilisation. But 'pretentious' was the wrong word, she said, it was feeble, 'impudent' might be a better word or perhaps 'hubris' would be best in this context, but it was also weak, much too weak, entirely too weak … 'Obscene,' that was the right word. The second reason, she said, was that she had the luxury to seek the right word, the time and ease, the time and space to think, and her brain at her beck and call, which made her self-disgust even stronger. Back then, he'd thought 'obscene' was overused and privately considered 'immoral' a better choice. But he hadn't said anything, he'd just listened as she described the film's protagonist, who she said was nothing like her. The film wasn't about the granddaughter of a perpetrator – though he knew, because they'd discussed it extensively, there were no real perpetrators in her family. (There hadn't even been a Nazi Party member in her family; there was only her grandfather, who'd been a soldier, strictly speaking a Mitläufer, a political hanger-on, a 22-year-old officer and troop commander in the 6th Army. And he had only survived Stalingrad because, shortly before reaching the city, after storming the Rostov airport, he had sustained a severe head injury. He'd received a so-called 'blighty wound' – a gift as it turned out, since it meant he was flown from the war zone to a field hospital in Hungary and released from combat duty post-convalescence. [After the capture of Rostov, the psychoanalyst, Sabina Spielrein, was murdered along with her two daughters in a mass execution. Graziela's grandfather hadn't been in an SS death squad and hadn't taken part in the shooting, but he had assisted in the capture of Rostov, and hence had brought about the murder of Sabina Spielrein. They had discussed all of this, specifically how it could be endured and whether it could be borne.]) *The Pawnbroker* was about an entirely different character, namely Sol Nazerman, a man burdened with survivor's guilt. (Rod Steiger, who played Nazerman, was nominated for an Oscar in 1966, as were Laurence Olivier for *Othello*, Oskar Werner for *Ship of Fools*, Richard Burton for *The Spy Who Came in from the Cold*, and Lee Marvin, who won Best Actor for his performance in *Cat Ballou*.) She could never forget the scene and it played instantly before her eyes whenever she was on a crowded train.

With that story, she'd planted the scene in him. He borrowed *The Pawnbroker* from the university's media centre and watched it once more at work on his Bureau's video recorder. After that, he too felt uneasy on every crowded train.

Now as he recalled this, he noticed that the uneasiness had disappeared, but he wasn't ashamed. In the past, he would have been thoroughly ashamed of himself for not being ashamed.

Not any more.

Now he could travel on an overcrowded train, even think about the people who had once been transported to the camps, and not feel ill. Now he could see birch trees and not think birch, Birke, 'Birkenau' – and he didn't believe it was because he'd become insensitive.

In the past, he had feared just this lack of sensitivity and was constantly on his guard. Over and over, he'd scrutinised and tested himself and decided he had undertaken every possible act of remembrance.

AUSCHWITZ LIVES IN EVERY SONG,
every flower, every tree.
Auschwitz lives in every song,
every German, including me.

Fiderallala, fiderallala, fideralla lala la.

HE WAS NOW PLAINLY USED TO HIS UNHAPPINESS. (Bless his post-war birth, ha ha.)

To his unhappiness he was now plainly used.

Fiderallala, fiderallala, fideralla lala la.

He wasn't certain when he'd got used to it, most likely after his thirtieth birthday – aeons ago. Perhaps when 'commemoration' was declared the official state duty. After that he no longer dared hope that his unhappiness would end, and so he no longer made the effort to end it. It existed like he existed – it was a part of him. He couldn't think about it any other way, couldn't imagine being without it; he lived with his unhappiness as a matter of course. Some people live in the countryside, others in the city, some have dark hair, others fair hair. Some have good fortune, others misfortune – that's the way it was. He belonged to those who lived with misery.

In the past he'd been able to laugh about it. And there was a lot to laugh about, because nothing went smoothly for him. He was a clown, clumsy, brooding over the smallest things, had no success with women, couldn't overcome his quirks, was always being barged into, and so on. In daily life he was a joke, but it was no longer funny to him. It was just too much effort. But in fact, the laughable things about him had not changed, only the most ridiculous thing about him. In the past his misery had had a concrete source. As long as he'd believed it stemmed from Auschwitz, his misery had substance. And the cause of his misery wasn't just the fact that Auschwitz had happened, it was his fixation with it. He thought constantly about what he could do and what the Auschwitz prisoners couldn't, and that Auschwitz had had a very different meaning for them than it did for him.

When he went to bed, for example, he thought about how they couldn't go to sleep when they wanted, how they'd had no beds, they'd had berths – that's what he thought about as he lay in his bed. Invariably his next thought was that there hadn't even been one berth per prisoner, whereas he couldn't recall when he'd last not slept alone in his own bed. Besides that, they weren't allowed to use the toilet when they needed to; they could only go at pre-scribed times and these were extremely brief, so their need was dire – that's what he thought about when he used the bathroom. Under the shower, he'd think about them being led to the 'sauna', as they had called it, and made to stand under a shower with temperatures they didn't control, suffering as the water switched from freezing cold to scalding hot.

All this.

For quite some time that had been his real affliction, the Auschwitz comparisons; and his obsession had worsened be-cause it was absurd. Eventually, his distress began to lessen. He had worked day-in and day-out in the vineyards of memory through the years, and perhaps this was the reason he no longer had to compare his every action to those of Auschwitz prison-ers. Throughout, he did whatever was in his power to relieve the survivors' misery: so that their suffering would never be repeated, and so that what had happened to them would never happen to anyone again.

Since that time, he saw no reason for his misery. Not in Ger-many.

Occasionally a terrible hatred of GERMANY overcame him, but it went by quickly. This hatred was intrinsic to the national character, and, he, Hans Frambach, was no less German than the others, even if he couldn't have precisely described what that was, where this essentially existed, this German-ness, (cf. Walter Abish, *How German Is It*. ©Walter Abish 1979, 1980, 1982). Whenever he was overwhelmed by self-loathing, he'd feel sud-denly young, and that was the real horror; it was suffocating to feel young and full of pure, righteous hate. He never wanted to be a boy again and was glad he had more than half his life behind him.

On the whole, he felt fine about Germany, at least the Germany he lived in.

He'd learned to differentiate the Germany he lived in from the era he worked on.

Really, he felt fine about Germany now. The public infrastructure functioned well, no one starved, fresh produce flowed without interruption, and corruption took place high up in executive suites, not at his low level where neither police nor doctors needed to be bribed.

What more do you want.

He had taken a long time to admit he liked his country. Once it would have seemed like a betrayal. Whenever he was asked why he worked at the Bureau of Past Management of all places and not in some more pleasant archive, he gave the same answer: he did it for the survivors, the elderly women and men with eyes as deep as drill holes, in which you couldn't, and didn't dare, look to the bottom. Moreover, they appeared so full of joie de vivre that he felt dead in comparison.

And yet he knew too well that there were some who'd survived the camps without an ounce of vitality left inside.

The survivors occasionally spoke of themselves in the past tense because most survivors were already dead. Those who weren't dead usually wanted nothing to do with his Bureau or any other memorial institution. And every day, there were fewer and fewer survivors.

No one had ever asked him the reason he'd chosen this occupation.

People used to go pale and silent when he responded to their questions about his work, whereas today they just nodded as if it were self-explanatory.

Memory work, right.

And then they changed the subject.

He'd already changed it.

At least it seemed to him that he'd changed it.

He went to the archive each day, carried out the work, preserving records and doing his duty.

He realised that concentration camp guards had given the exact same answer when they were asked why they'd done that job, of all things, and not some other. If nothing else, they'd all been taught what it meant to be German, which was to do a thing for its own sake. (*Here came to consciousness and received its plain expression, what G e r m a n is: to wit, the thing one does for its own sake, for the very joy of doing it; whereas Utilitarianism, namely, the principle whereby a thing is done for the sake of some personal end, ulterior to the thing itself, was shown to be un-German.* Wagner, Richard. *Prose Works, Art and Politics.* Tr. by William Ashton Ellis, vol. 4, p. 107, Kegan, Paul, Trench, Trübner & Co, Ltd., 1895, London.) Furthermore, he'd been taught to question everything critically, and foremost, his German-ness. (Though he hadn't been taught to consider the reference to joy in this citation.) His discomfort at the loss of his unease stemmed from his German-ness because if he questioned its loss, he would have to recognise that he was another self-loathing German. He had become another prison guard, and it didn't bother him any longer. *They dwindle, they fall / the suffering people* … (Hölderlin, Friedrich. *Hyperion or The Hermit in Greece.* Vol. II, ii. [*Hyperion to Bellarmin,* 'Hyperion's Song of Destiny']). And while he could no longer refer to a specific, concrete cause, his misery remained, and he

gave himself over to it.

The misery, as natural to him as breathing, was large, immeasurably larger than he, and yet it was completely dependent on him; if he did not exist – he prided himself, in comparatively happy moments – the misery would have no host animal. Actually, he knew the misery couldn't care less about him and was as independent as it could be. But if there were no misery, he'd be nothing – he lived only with and on misery. Without misery he would have been unable to define himself. It was never his; in reality it didn't belong to him. It was not his misery but

The Misery.

If he removed it from himself, nothing of him would remain, nothing. Utterly nothing. (He knew this. But it was no use to him.)

TODAY, AS HE RECALLED THIS, he wondered if Graziela still dwelled on the scene while travelling on crowded trains and if she thought of those people transported in cattle cars to barracks, barracks that had been designed as stables for Wehrmacht horses. Every time he remembered, he resolved to ask her, but he always forgot. Nowadays, they rarely spoke about Auschwitz, and when they did, their tone was dry and factual. It wasn't the way they had once spoken, with a lump in their throats and feeling they were at an abyss.

In any event, they saw each other much less often than they once had.

New week, same old misery. He took the lift to the 16th floor of the Bureau of Past Management, held his plastic ID to the designated spot by the entrance until he heard a quiet click, opened the door and stepped into the archive's familiar reception area – a cube of cold light. Above him the ceiling's fluorescent strip buzzed insistently, lighting up every corner of the room so that Frau Kermer's perfectly styled blonde hair gleamed like ice. It flowed down to her elbows and, because she made certain never to let her hair get out of place, she sometimes looked like a statue, a glistening reception Buddha. But mostly like a dragon at the mouth of a cave. Or the guardian of the Grail. And sometimes like the Beast of Buchenwald.

He drew up the corners of his mouth so she would think he was smiling. There would be no other choice. He observed all social conventions, which was why he pulled up the corners – it was customary, that's how people smiled.

'Good morning, Frau Kermer,' he said, turning at once to the coat rack to let the corners of his mouth drop to where they belonged. She addressed her greeting to his back as he hung his coat with elaborate care. Sliding a hanger into the shoulders symmetrically, he then put the hanger on the pole, paying even closer attention so that his coat hung as freely as possible – barely touching the wall and certainly not Frau Kermer's, which already hung there. He bent down, tucked his briefcase – which he'd gripped between his legs – under his left arm, and, standing once again, pressed the case to his belly while combing down his hair with his right hand. Frau Kermer must have been watching because she threw her grappling hook after him just as he turned away.

'Herr Frambach!' she called, dragging him off-kilter, and as she spoke, he couldn't prevent the corners of his mouth from sliding up. It was automatic.

'Herr Marschner asked if you would keep eleven-thirty free. He'd like very much to speak to you.'

Frambach nodded.

'When will he arrive?' he said, simply to stretch out the conversation and relax the corners of his mouth.

'Around eleven,' said Frau Kermer. Frambach nodded once more. The smile, which Frau Kermer did not mirror, hurt him, pushing itself ever more firmly into his face. Naturally, Marschner knew it didn't matter what time they met during work hours. It would be highly unlikely not to meet in the office during those hours, particularly because Frambach sat faithfully at his desk from early until late, feeding one document after another into the archive, and had no meetings outside the office; Marschner nevertheless scheduled meetings in advance, always asking Frau Kermer to make the appointments. It was his way of giving an overall impression of urgency and professionalism. And it was very successful.

The heavy creases on Frau Kermer's forehead tilted her face back down in the direction of her desk. Her paperwork always seemed of utmost importance, as if it couldn't tolerate the slightest delay. She had not responded to his smile, and consequently it had not waned, which was why, as he entered the dim corridor that led to his office, he shook himself to hurl the smile from his face. He clutched his bag with both arms and gave himself a shake, short but sharp, a quick but powerful shake to get rid of his idiotic smile. Now it lay in the dark on the already cluttered floor among all the other smiles he'd forced every morning to greet Frau Kermer. The cleaning woman casually swept his smiles into the corners, but she couldn't remove them because she didn't have the proper machine.

The Bureau of Past Management is situated in the centre of Berlin, a large city sprawled against the flat landscape. Compared to other cities in Germany, it's not very old; actually, it's fairly new. Nonetheless, full of history. History has battered this large city with heavy hammers time and again, and you can see it – precisely because the city sought to shake off, make smaller, clear away whatever had been created in bygone eras. That desire to shake off, make smaller, clear away is the city's trademark, as one resident recognised long ago, prophesying that Berlin was 'damned always to become, and never to be,' (cf. Karl Scheffler, Berlin, *Ein Stadtschicksal*. 1910. *Berlin –The Psychogramme of a City*. Tr. by Michael Hofmann, Berlin: Suhrkamp Verlag, 2021). The city has honestly fulfilled its fate. And history didn't just leave a wasteland behind, it left grand edifices as well.

At sixteen storeys high and nearly four hundred feet wide, the Bureau's office building was erected by the East Germans during the city's most recently completed historic period, and instead of being razed to the ground, it was completely renovated. Six lifts ascend and descend the floors at once, carrying people up and down, yet the Bureau's employees often have to wait for a free lift. Why? The Bureau has innumerable employees. They need vast numbers of people because the past, which they manage, is itself vast; they aren't rolling a single boulder into the future like Sisyphus did, but a mountain of rubble.

Everyone who works here meets regularly, without an appointment, on the eighth floor in the middle of the building – if it's considered vertically. That's where the cafeteria is. Here you can enter freely, and without a plastic ID card, for the doors are always open. However, you can't buy anything without the plastic card and, before purchasing, you have to put money onto that card.

The machine used for transferring monetary value to the card is a small rectangular block with two slots. The card goes in one slot, the money in the other. That's what the machine eats, but very reluctantly. Regardless of the value, the machine spits out the money many times over before finally slurping it down. Due to the machine's reluctance to transfer value as advertised onto an anonymous plastic card, which is to say, to transfer the value of one thing onto another thing, this little machine is the heartbeat of the building in the very heart of the capital city where the country's past and future histories meet. Right here, historic events are carefully documented and evaluated, and despite being made tangible, at any given point the exact value of these events remains incomprehensible, even when the past seems within one's grip.

At the beginning, the Bureau's work wasn't fruitful or relevant, but gradually over the years it became as necessary for people as air to breathe. The Bureau's mission, which was to research historical narratives and cultivate an understanding of the nation's history, would forge a path for the future, and that research would help organise what would become the state, which had risen from that very history.

Eventually all of the nation's institutions became involved in the memorialisation of the historic crime. What had begun slowly, gained speed. After the nation became a sovereign state (the partition having been the direct consequence of the crime) and was no longer at the forefront of the Cold War, it could then, finally, begin to concern itself solely with itself. Now the state was no longer responsible to other states for its actions, only to the people who had managed to survive, who had neither institutions nor armies. These people had only the memories of the terrible things that had been done to them by representatives of the German people, though not by the present state. Now those people were very old. There were also some people alive, not many, who had perpetrated the crime. For them, it was a faded memory. They were very old now, too.

Most of the nation's living citizens were not yet born when the crime happened, or had been, at most, merely children. All the same, the monstrosity of their forebears' crime weighed heavily on them, and when they approached this monstrosity, they expected nothing but to unmask their forebears and find criminals. They proceeded without hindrance – it was a continuous loop. The crime was so large. So enormous it would continue into the seventh generation.

The ongoing revelations of their forebears' crime were disturbing, but necessary; after the disclosures no longer seemed necessary, they were even more unpleasant. Given that, the state remembered its duty and resolved to take this burden away from its citizens; it would undertake to memorialise the crime as its eternal duty. It would cast the burden into historical monuments to fulfil the obligation; and, as years went by, the number of monuments increased, and yet the crime did not diminish – it could not be left behind. Every place where the crime had occurred, and there were many, was designated a memorial site. Commemoration was no longer regarded merely as a necessity, but also as the nation's most noble duty, and there was no more honourable place to work than at the Bureau of Past Management, which was located in the capital, because this was where, officially, the heart of the nation beat. (Of course, only the Bureau's headquarters occupied the building; its many subsidiaries were spread throughout the nation.)

And over time, the state crawled out from the darkness, which was subjected to the brightest light. The darkness was an essential aspect of the state and it was only logical, therefore, that the darkness became the reason for the state's foundation.

It was understood.

It was no secret and needn't be discussed.

It was The Essential.

Except that the crime was no longer of interest when it was served up on a large platter and lit on all sides by a thousand suns. From the Blitzkrieg, the Blitz Light was born, and the reality of the crime became a tale from bygone days.

He knew that too. And yet the knowledge didn't help him in this case either because he couldn't help being obsessed with the crime.

It was such a large crime.

Shocking now that it hardly hurt. That was the essential horror: for to him this was the essential thing. That this crime, which was so enormous, could have stopped hurting. That that was possible. That such a thing is possible – it was terrible. And that amplified his misery.

He felt like someone who had dropped out of time. It hurt him to this very day.

No sooner had he entered his office, than the telephone began to buzz. The ringer, turned as low as possible, made the phone sound as if it were complaining, as if no one noticed the way it did its duty like a zealot. But that wasn't true. He would never leave it to ring unanswered and didn't today. He didn't even set his briefcase down before going straight to his desk, where he picked up the receiver and saw Frau Kermer's name on the display.

'Yes.'

'Frau Schönbluhm phoned five minutes ago,' said Frau Kermer.

'Yes,' he said again.

'I told her you'd be arriving shortly.'

'Yes, of course,' and he put the receiver down, turning to place his briefcase on the visitor's chair near the door. He then switched on his computer monitor and watched the programs greet the new workday with a long, happy jig, letting him know they existed now and forever, assuring him that today, as always, they functioned wholly and irreproachably and could be called upon to obey every order, would be able and willing to follow without hesitation any imaginable, as well as designated command (which was a lie). Finally, the many small windows opened, and he logged on with his username and password. The telephone grumbled once more. Seeing Graziela's number on the display, he picked up: 'I'll call right back – haven't had coffee –' and hung up.

His briefcase sat peacefully on the extra chair by the door, but something was amiss. He stared, wondering why the wall looked so bare. The telephone grumbled. Graziela's number again. He picked up the receiver quickly, hung up, picked it up again, dialled five, and put the receiver down near the phone. He questioned if he shouldn't end their friendship after these many years, but realised suddenly that that wouldn't be possible – he'd have absolutely no one to talk to – and, at last, recognised why the wall by the door looked bare: his coat wasn't on the hook where it belonged.

Frau Kermer watched with anticipation. This time he didn't smile at her as he took his coat from the hanger on the rack, turned, went back to his room and hung his coat on the hook near his door so that the coat covered the chair's back. Its hem grazed the seat and the briefcase leaned against it, holding the coat in place; if the door opened and a draft blew into the room, the coat wouldn't move. Everything was as it should be. For now, everything was all right.

Graziela looked like Picasso had painted her, like one of Picasso's portraits of Dora Maar. Except in Graziela's case it wasn't art; she was larger than art and larger than nature. She just looked like art.

She had big eyes, a big nose and a big mouth, and the single elements of her face were arranged as if they weren't connected to each other in any reasonable proportion, so you couldn't form an opinion of them.

The nose was slightly askew. From its point of view, it slanted to the right, from the onlooker's, to the left.

Her eyes drooped somewhere under her forehead. They were greyish blue.

Her big mouth had almost no colour; you only noticed it when she spoke, rather like an oddly textured shape moving around an opening in her face. When she didn't speak, her mouth was lost in the rough sketch that served as her countenance.

When they'd first met, he thought a lot about Graziela's face and couldn't decide whether she was very ugly or unusually beautiful. He stared at her unabashedly whenever they were together, and she stared unabashedly back, all the while describing the various aspects of her personal suffering, which had stemmed from the Nazi era.

Once when he went with her to the symphony (Ludwig van Beethoven's Symphony No. 1 C-major (Op. 21) edition, Jonathan Del Mar; Anton Webern's *Six Pieces for Orchestra* (Op. 6b) version 1928; Ludwig van Beethoven's Symphony No. 7 A-major (Op. 92) edition, Jonathan Del Mar), he'd seen her made-up for the first time (she'd met Joachim by then). She'd bathed her lips in blood, bolted down her eyes with kohl and heavy mascara, and turned her face into an Expressionist painting – which you couldn't enter, because right in the middle her big nose pointed you in the wrong direction.

How could anyone walk around looking like that!

Unfortunately, you couldn't divide the letters of her first name by three. He tried it automatically each time she popped into his mind, but he failed of course; her name could only be divided perfectly by three if it was combined with her last name, which was somewhat reassuring. However, he couldn't constantly think of her by her whole name as if hers were the name of an SS Sturmbannführer in some file or other.

For him, she was Graziela, unfortunately eight letters, and eight was not divisible by three, and there was nothing to do about it. The rule of three worked for Graziela only by combining her name with something that was a genuine part of her and that could be divided by three. 'Eyes,' 'nose,' 'lips,' didn't fit. 'Cheeks' worked. 'Gra-zie-la's che-eks' pleased him because it was fifteen letters, his favourite number of letters, and when he divided it by three, he got five. That was orderly, workable, and could be no other way: fifteen divided by three equals five, five times three equals fifteen – a won-der-ful thing.

People were a hardship for him, and people whose names couldn't be divided by three were his first hurdle. (Frau Kermer, whose first name was Elisabeth, was an obvious exception. Perhaps it was because he would never have called her by her first name, and only referred to her as 'Frau Kermer'; the extra letter being the measure by which she would forever lack his affection.)

Graziela's face was beyond simple aesthetic appreciation. When you think about it, if you know someone over a long period, even if you don't know that person well, she no longer looks ugly. But also not beautiful. Ugly and beautiful stop being meaningful distinctions. Hans decided to find her face as beautiful as her body, which made him think less of Picasso and more of

Botero, for it was firm and round and large like everything about her; her breasts were just extra pillows in the fleshy body she wore every day.

It should have been comfortable to walk around in Graziela's magnificent body. There was so much room, every imaginable state of mind could collapse onto her body's soft cushions and not be hurt, but for Graziela, who theoretically had exclusive possession of it, the exact opposite was true. She didn't observe herself with the eye of an art connoisseur; she thought her face was ugly and her body just plain fat. She was like the old West Germany.

Lucky for her, she'd won the lottery – or so she thought when someone became interested in her body – and his name was Joachim. He wasn't merely into her body; he was thrilled by it (he really was) and was aroused whenever he thought about it. It excited an extreme hunger in him, along with the knowledge that his appetite would be totally satisfied asap. He said repeatedly to Graziela, owner and resident of this body, how incredible it was, and because Graziela had never known anyone who'd expressed any particular joy for her body, she immediately placed it at his disposal – meaning she gave it to him with no limit on time or activity, and since then had begun to feel friendlier toward her outward appearance.

Ever since Joachim had begun to desire her body, Graziela had looked in the mirror without thinking about dieting, and she tried to imagine what he saw. To be honest, she still failed to see how her body was beautiful, although he told her blatantly that it was, but at least she felt content. Without it, she reasoned, she wouldn't have a lover. She no longer judged her face by contemporary aesthetic norms and focused instead on making herself more attractive, always making up her face and grooming herself carefully to keep her body primed She washed more frequently and used expensive cream on her skin, shaved her legs even in winter, and went to a hair salon regularly; in good conscience, she ate chocolate but also more vegetables than before, and she drank many litres of water, so that the substance of her body would stay as healthy and fresh as possible. Now that someone coveted her body, it had become important. Graziela believed that their affair, hers and Joachim's, had been reduced to its purist kernel, rendered down to its essence; and, moreover, she believed that the total reduction offered the greatest fulfilment.

The whole point was to be flesh, nothing else. Her love would consist of nothing more, would have no feature other than sex, none of the other elements that made each person unique; love, she believed, could be known solely by her sex, a common characteristic, and only through its most obvious trait; all others were deemed irrelevant. To be a woman and nothing else. To sing with Carole King, or better yet, with Aretha Franklin:

> *You make me feel*
> *You make me feel*
> *You make me feel like a na-tu-ral woman,*

one of the stupidest pop songs ever.

The whole point of love was stripped down to one unique element, which in reality was nothing special. Something special was just the stripping down.

Although Hans wasn't aware of all of this, he'd seen how she behaved and had changed since Joachim entered her life. It hadn't been lost on him – the way she now groomed herself, dressed elegantly, always with freshly washed hair, always smelling of perfume and talking about 'relationship issues' instead of Auschwitz. Back when Graziela wore jeans and sweatshirts and talked about Auschwitz, he'd thought she understood his misery because she shared it. That's how they'd become friends. They'd never spoken about her own misery, her own specific unhappiness – it had

29

been unimportant in light of the immense, vast misfortune they had constantly discussed. That was before she had switched sides and believed she was happy with her so-called relationship.

He'd met this Joachim a few times – the letters of his name were not only indivisible by three, they also added up to the ugliest sum – when he'd arrived precisely as Joachim was leaving. Graziela always looked velvety, as if she'd been massaged, and Joachim positively sunny, which made Hans want to vomit. Thereafter he avoided meeting Joachim whenever possible. Once he ran into him in passing just as Joachim was saying goodbye to Graziela, and he came away from their meeting feeling somehow insulted. Now, if he and Graziela were meeting at her place, he always made sure to ask whether she'd be seeing Joachim before or after, and if so, he arrived late or left early, or proposed another date right away.

HE TOOK HIS COFFEE MUG FROM HIS OFFICE CABINET where he put it after washing it each evening, shut his door and went to the kitchen where Frau Kermer's coffee-machine-brewed coffee was already bitter. All the other offices were open and the rooms empty. The graduate student was in the library, there were no interns around at the moment, and Marschner would surely not arrive until eleven. It was very peaceful in the archives. Only the door to the computer room at the end of the corridor was closed.

The computer room was The Essential to the Bureau of Past Management's archive, an interconnected meta-archive, and it created central access to the various archives and documents needed for the cultivation and management of the past. The Bureau's archive was tiny and held only newfound material, unexpected discoveries, curiosities. In truth, Frambach's daily tasks only amounted to a memory of archival science, an embellishment that one wouldn't want to part with for nostalgic reasons, itself a form of managing the past. He had no contact with the people who worked in the computer room. They lived on another planet, only to be glimpsed on their way to lunch, always together, never mingling with the others. Without fail they materialised immediately if he had a problem with his computer, fixed it in two minutes at most, accepted his thanks with quiet contempt, and scurried back to their mainframe computer. He was, in effect, alone with Frau Kermer.

He poured into his coffee thick sweetened and pasteurised cream from the little bottle that sat on his desk, and called Graziela, who was already on the phone before he'd heard the ring.

'Oh Hans,' she said. 'I'm so sorry, I have to cancel tonight.'

He pressed his lips together hard, making a facial expression that differed only slightly from a smile. Then he once again loosened his lips and said from the back of his throat, 'Joachim.'

'Yes. Joachim suddenly has time tonight, and I haven't seen him in a week.'

'Yes,' he said, and thought of how he hadn't seen Graziela in two weeks.

They were silent for a moment.

'Fine. Or not fine. Let's talk later, I have work to do.'

'I'm really sorry.'

'It's okay. Bye.' And he hung up.

On the outside he was cold, and inside he was empty. He stared at the equally empty little windows on his monitor screen. There was a lump in his throat he didn't want to swallow. He typed an abbreviation of his own name, 'hafram,' in the upper window, and the Auschwitz SS Commander's, 'hoess,' in the lower. The Bureau's archival program welcomed him, and he took the next document from the box with Siegfried Wolkenkraut's posthumous papers to enter into the archive's primary research files.

ACCOUNT
OF
MY
TIME IN
SEVERAL
CONCENTRATION CAMPS

At the end of January 1943
I was
deported
from Theresienstadt to
Auschwitz–Birkenau.

I
had lived
in Theresienstadt
with my parents
for one year.

My parents were
only deported to
Auschwitz
in October 1944
and
immediately
murdered there
in the gas chamber.

I was
deemed fit for work

at the selection on arrival in
Auschwitz and therefore
was not
immediately
murdered
in the gas chamber.

In camp
I
survived
later
selections,
moreover
the death march
to evacuate
Auschwitz in
December 1944, which brought me to
Bergen–Belsen.

From there
British troops
freed us
in April 1945.
Today
I live
in Lower Saxony near Northeim in the village of
Imbshausen.

I work
as a hand on a farmstead.

I am
a lithographer and poet.

THE SHEET OF PAPER WAS UNDATED. It was already the forty-sixth document with this exact same text. Frambach stamped it with the Bureau's official stamp and wrote the archive number on the line provided. On the screen he typed the number in the table and wrote in the column 'Title': 'Account of my time in several concentration camps'; in the column 'Style': 'account'; in the column 'Size': '1 leaf, 1 p.'; in the column 'Description': 'good cond., typescript, n.d.'; and in the column 'Comments': 'sharply broken lines.'

There were also handwritten versions of this same account. The individual versions showed no variation in content whatsoever; there were only those without line breaks, in quasi-prose, and ones like this, with lines broken in a quasi-lyric form. Wolkenkraut had never dated these reports, so it was impossible to establish whether he would have broken the lines more sharply over time or found his way to a continuous text.

WOLKENKRAUT'S PAPERS HAD BEEN MISSING FOR A LONG TIME. However, no one at the Bureau of Past Management lamented the missing estate, because the few examples of his abilities he'd produced in his short life were not promising and hadn't caught anyone's attention. Apart from a slim volume of verse published in 1951 ('with three illustrations by the author'), plus two short essays that appeared that same year in a Lower Saxon local paper, he'd had no publications, and his lithography had been exhibited only once, in a now-closed gallery in Göttingen, as evidenced by a little catalogue. In March 1953, Siegfried Wolkenkraut was run over by a tractor in Imbshausen near Northeim and died at the scene of the accident. He was twenty-nine years old and was survived by a wife and daughter. What became of them had been no one's concern until a wooden box with his belongings arrived at the Bureau. In all likelihood, Wolkenkraut's wife was no longer alive, otherwise she would have inherited the box; probably only the daughter, Mafalda, had remained – and she left no one behind in Schweinfurt when she jumped from the 12th-floor balcony of her apartment. She had placed a note on the box requesting that it be sent to the Bureau of Past Management. Nothing else. No further explanation, also no suicide note, according to the Probate Court's notification letter.

HE TOOK THE NEXT DOCUMENT, placed it in front of him, read
and turned it over, read the back, turned it again, stamped it,
gave it a number and typed into the computer the title he'd cop-
ied from the preceding entry: 'Account of my time in several
concentration camps, account, 1 leaf, moderate condition, handwritten, paper creased, n.d., verso: price list Merzenbach Co.
(milking pails, pitchforks), d. 1.VII.1948; unbroken lines' and
placed the sheet upside down on the left tab of the portfolio,
where the first already lay.

The date of the price list on the back was a clue, but not a
reliable one. How long would a price list like this lie around a
farm until it was unneeded and thrown away? Wouldn't a price
list be valid for quite some time? How important were new milk
pails and pitchforks? Surely there would have been a few already
on hand. After the currency reform, had there been money to
invest in such things immediately, or had there been something
else more important?

*I WALK INTO EVENING and, in complete surrender, I lay my head
under night's slaughtering axe.*
No title (I walk into evening), note, 1 leaf, 1p.,
poor condition, handwritten, n.d.

Marschner's good mood whirled around like a carousel swing, and he was the pole in the middle. If he made a slight movement, the carousel made a larger one; and so the empty swings flew on long chains in a wide circle around him, clanging against walls, doors and cabinets, upsetting all the cups, and crashing into windowpanes. Wherever Marschner appeared there reigned a flurry of noise and sudden commotion. He was such a noisy person that Frambach could hear him at the entrance from a distance of thirty feet, even though he sat at his desk behind his closed door. He heard Marschner recount an anecdote about today's hunt for a parking spot, the long search ending in an escapade – no doubt he was trying to amuse Frau Kermer, which had seemed to work because her shrill laughter scissored again and again through the deep tones of Marschner's monologue. Then came an almost peaceful moment, only a murmur, probably while Frau Kermer reported what had happened since yesterday afternoon, what was in the mail, and who had phoned. Then once more, Marschner's fairground-trumpet-and-clang until Frau Kermer's chainsaw laughter united with Marschner's heavy steps, accompanying him another moment.

Frambach heard Marschner rumbling near and prepared for his boss's appearance. In general, he barely paused at Frambach's door, but after a quick knock, he tore open the door to the cosy room, filling it to bursting with his fervour and carousel jangling.

'Good morning!' shouted Marschner as he squeezed Frambach's shoulder. 'Everything as it should be?'

Of course, how else would it be?

The computer worked, the coffee tasted terrible, Wolkenkraut wrote the same passage on and on.

'I'd like to speak to you.'

'I know, Frau Kermer has already told me.'

'Would half past eleven be alright with you?'

'Yes, I've reserved the time.' Frambach gave in,

Frambach gave back,

Frambach gave over to protocol,

while Marschner studied his watch and shouted, 'Jeez! It's late! I have to handle a couple of calls, but then, wow, I've got wonderful news for you!' Once more, he squeezed Hans's shoulder before stomping out, leaving the door ajar. Hans closed it again straight away. 'A couple of calls' meant a minimum of five anyway. What it also meant was that their meeting would take place at noon at the earliest, more likely twelve thirty, and although Marschner was never punctual, and although Hans knew this and knew, too, the precise extent of Marschner's chronic lateness, he let himself be disappointed and already felt anxious shortly before eleven thirty when Frau Kermer called, asking him to be patient. But he was restless, couldn't concentrate, and stared constantly at the clock.

HE KNEW ALL THIS, TOO, but it did him no good. At any moment of the day he could tell you precisely what mistakes he was making and how those mistakes stemmed from his unhappiness, and how his unhappiness stuck to him and was worsening; and, conversely, how his unhappiness stemmed from his mistakes and was also worsening, and how this had become a habit that would continue for eternity – he knew this precisely, but it did him no good.

He called Graziela. After saying hello, he explained how he was supposed to have a meeting with Marschner at eleven thirty but it had been delayed, as she must have already perceived since it was eleven thirty-seven, and he guessed the meeting wouldn't take place until twelve thirty, which meant he had plenty of time to talk now – and so he asked, how are things?

Of course, this question was superfluous, things were unusually well owing to her date that evening with Joachim – her whole life revolved around the man – who, it seemed, had less control of his schedule than he would have liked, because of his obligations as a husband and family man. If Hans had ever considered an amorous relationship with Graziela for other than practical reasons, and if their friendship had not been atom-bomb proof, and if they had not been like siblings from the start, he would have been jealous for other reasons and not just frequently annoyed, and would have ended their friendship long ago. But Joachim had never been a threat. Quite the contrary. Since Joachim's appearance in her life, Graziela had had more to talk to him about. Instead of discussing how their grandparents and nationality had entrenched them in Germany's terrible history, they analysed, interpreted, and assessed Joachim's every comment, combing through his confusing conversation for some possible consolation, and considered how best to soothe his trivial irritations. The need was always urgent and existential, and Hans had asked himself more than twice if he could really play the role she'd cast him in. When she'd shared the fruits of her reading – from a woman's magazine – it had become clear to him that he was as good as buried in the role, entombed as in the concrete walls of an anti-aircraft bunker. Statistically speaking, the article stated, the status of an extra-marital affair remains the same unless the adulterer separates from his or her spouse within the first year of the affair. Graziela had nurtured her bond to, relationship with, and dependence on Joachim for roughly four years.

However, she'd let Hans know he'd become more important to her since she'd met Joachim, even if that barely seemed possible. She'd begun reading *Le Coup de grâce* by Marguerite Yourcenar (*The Coup de Grâce*. 1939. Tr. by Grace Frick) though after the first three pages, she told him the book was a total slog. That said, on page fourteen, she found the sentence:

Friendship affords certitude above all, and that is what distinguishes it from love.

She quoted this to him and said the book had given her so much already that she didn't need to finish it. Then she repeated the sentence, remarking that it was worth the whole book.

At that he'd almost wept. (Thank you, Marguerite Yourcenar!)

He went straight away to buy a copy to read again, because he couldn't remember the passage. He didn't tell Graziela – that would have been obnoxious, or so he thought. This time he read the book in the original, and not only to the sentence:

L'amitie est avant tout certitude, c'est ce que la distingue de l'amour,

but to the very last page, to pay his debt of gratitude to Marguerite Yourcenar, although he thought it was a disagreeable novel. What fascinated the French about Baltic nobility, German military and war in East Prussia, he'd never understand – he simply noted it. He didn't think about Germany as he once had, that is to say, he thought about it much less often. Nevertheless, he was disturbed that a woman had written such a woman-hating book.

'Everything's fine,' said Graziela as expected, 'and you?'
  'The usual misery,' he answered.
  'Well then, everything's all right.'

'LISTEN, HANS,' she went on, 'I'm really sorry to cancel this evening, but maybe you'd like to come to an organ concert with me on Friday evening?'

'Organ concert.'

'Yes. Actually six little concerts, one after another. In a church. I have to look at the space and check the acoustics. One of my students suggested we hold our next recital there. She's a member of the congregation. We needn't stay the whole time.'

'No.'

'No? You won't come with me?'

'No, I meant, "No, we needn't stay the whole time." Of course I'll come with you.' I'll go anywhere with you, he thought but didn't say, wherever you'll take me. Of course I'll come with you – anything's better than being at home, sitting there alone.

'That's great,' said Graziela. 'Let's discuss the details later. I can't talk now. I should get going – my first student's at one.'

'Fine.' Meanwhile it was just eleven thirty-eight and he had fifty-two minutes to kill.

'I'll call this evening.'

'I thought you were seeing Joachim tonight.'

'Yes, I'm seeing Joachim, but he won't stay forever. I'll call you when he leaves.'

'Okay, fine,' he said once more, and this time he meant it sincerely, without irony; now he could look forward to their late-night chat. The day wouldn't end with nothing, now it would have a finale. After all. That was no small thing.

'ALTHOUGH OUR ARCHIVE is the smallest department in the Bureau of Past Management, you know it is of the highest importance,' began Marschner.

'Yes,' said Frambach, waiting for what would certainly follow, namely Marschner's extensive self-promotion: how he'd led the archive to its current technical perfection ('state-of-the-art'); how, if not for him, it would still be accessed by index cards ('manual system'); whereas now all of the innumerable managers of the past could access the farthest flung records without any difficulty whatsoever, and with seamless efficiency, because now there were no far-flung records; how Marschner, through constant successful solicitations from government sources, of course, but also from private institutions from whom he'd raised significant funds ('public-private partnerships'), had placed at the archive's disposal the best, the most fabulous information centre ('central computer facilities') of any contemporary German archive ('state of the art').

Frambach knew all this, not only because Marschner pointed it out frequently, but because he'd been working there for a number of years. He also knew that after the boasts about the Bureau's technical facilities and financial endowment, a hint would follow that without Marschner's ongoing, successful money-raising (*das Fundraising*), his own job would no longer be needed (*das Outsourcing*), and that only Marschner could prevent that outcome.

'Fortunately,' Frambach said, as he always did, though for some time he hadn't known if it was fortunate. At least Marschner's name could be divided by three.

'And now guess where you'll be going in two weeks,' said Marschner.

Frambach steadied himself for the worst.

'To Shanghai!' shrieked Marschner. 'Isn't that amazing?!'

To Shanghai?

He sensed that his face had become a smooth sheet of glass. Shanghai ranked nowhere on the scale of the terrible things he was prepared for; he hadn't even considered Shanghai. He didn't know what to think. Was it amazing or not? Certainly it was far away. And at least he could divide Yan-gtz-e Ri-ver by three.

He was petrified, and that was the worst thing. Amazing. Far away. What could he say to that? Terrific? He was clueless, he knew nothing at all, and so he couldn't take his eyes off Marschner. As if Marschner could help him. But Marschner couldn't. And besides, he noticed, he was staring right through Marschner.

'Hey, aren't you happy about it?' said Marschner. He reached forward and thumped Frambach's shoulder with his large paw, then leaned back in his chair (they were in the so-called *conference facilities* used for important discussions) and laughed so loud that the carousel swing, now nearly horizontal, flew in a circle. Frambach ducked.

'I've surprised you, eh?' Marschner laughed. Then he held the thumb of his outstretched hand to his nose and linked the pinkie finger to the thumb of his other hand, wiggling the fingers of both hands. Thunderstruck, Hans stared at him. Luckily Marschner took his hands away from his nose immediately and slapped his thighs. Hans knew that this gesture, 'to thumb your nose,' was known in other places, England among them, as 'the Shanghai gesture,' (cf. Archer Taylor: *The Shanghai Gesture*. Helsinki, Finland 1956. [Suomalainen Tiedeakatemia/Academia Scientiarum Fennica. FF Communications No. 166]).

He wondered whether Marschner knew the reference, too, and if that was the reason he'd thumbed his nose at him.

The question came to his rescue, relaxing his face somewhat so that he could speak again. Suddenly his mouth spoke of its own accord.

47

'Indeed, this is quite a surprise,' he said.

'And what am I to do in Shanghai?' he asked,

as if he didn't know about the emigration to Shanghai,

as if he didn't suspect there was so-called treasure to be found; completely unknown or hitherto lost, but valid estates to examine,

as if he didn't dread having another project to initiate, further cooperation between the Bureau of Past Management and a foreign institution with who-knew-what reputation,

as if it weren't completely clear to him that Marschner, whose egregious activity never paused for anything, would again strike it rich, literally, in a far-flung location.

He thought he'd acted his part perfectly, playing innocent and not letting Marschner ruin his day. All the same, he was surprised Marschner didn't want to travel to Shanghai himself, and suspected there was actual work to be done, and that it wouldn't be pretty.

The Management of the Past

I. The Hooked Crossroads

In an effort to discuss historic land consolidation, our first point will be the Hooked Crossroads (aka the Swasti-crossroads), the place we Germans stumbled terribly in our march through history, where our elders chose the wrong road – the path that led to our downfall, not the future.

We begin with a factual description of the subject and shall discuss it immediately after.

Proposal for the description of the Hooked Crossroads, sentence 1:

Suddenly the road makes a sharp bend.

Discussion:

> A: Hmm, 'sharp bend' is well put. But isn't it more the case that the road makes a classic ninety-degree angle and suddenly turns a corner?
> B: Sorry, but I'm not sure an angle can be called 'classic'.
> A: Why not? Why can't an angle be called classic?
> B: Come on, an angle? It's simple geometry – it's just the way it is.
> A: Yes indeed! And so it has been from time immemorial. It was, is, will remain so. Ergo, classic - just as I said!
> B *(grumpily)*: All right then, if you insist, let's move on: the road makes a sudden sharp bend.

A: Yes, the road makes a sudden sharp bend, then one goes around the corner, and –

B: What now? A sharp bend or a corner? First you say bend, now you say corner.

A: But what difference does it make?

B: Very simple, very, very simple: a corner is a ninety-degree angle, and a bend could be anything. A corner is THE classic ninety-degree angle.

A: That's exactly what I said initially, and you totally disagreed. You said there was no such a thing as a classic angle. Only a classic bend would do.

B: I NEVER SAID THAT!

Pause.

A: Will you listen to me now?

B: Yes, only try to sound less like a classic stuffed shirt!

A: THE ONLY THING CLASSIC HERE IS YOUR INTOLERENCE!

B: That fits the subject.

A: TRUE ENOUGH! It's the one thing we have left, intolerance! PEOPLE LIKE YOU AND YOUR NARROW-MINDEDNESS! Poor Germany, that's all I can say, poor Germany!

B: What are you talking about? 'Poor Germany?' What's that supposed to mean? Perhaps that's one of your 'classic' (!!!) expressions? Hmm? Now you're showing your true colours! You of all people should avoid that expression! The fact that you! used! that! precise! expression! for this! precise! subject! Precisely you! Precisely this expression! If this is one of your CATCHPHRASES , you ought to know you won't get away with it, no way, absolutely not, and don't say anything more. Nothing! Don't speak to me!

We see the two blubbering like speared sausages, speckled with insulted slobber and blood split as they seethe into the sunset.

II. The Meat Hook

> GROUP A: Fascist pigs!
> GROUP B: Communist cows!
> GROUP A: Informers!
> GROUP B: Idiots!
> GROUP A: Hypocrites, deniers, liars!
> GROUP B: Cry-babies!
> GROUP A: Perpetrators!
> GROUP B: Traitors!
> GROUP A: Murderers!
> GROUP B: Terrorists!
> GROUP A: We don't want you here! Just get out! Disappear! Go to hell where you belong!
> GROUP B: Huh? You think we wanted you, you vipers in the nest, you ungrateful brats?! Do you think we wanted you?! We'll cut you down to size!
> GROUP A: You won't cut us down! We're young – we're the future. The future is ours. You'll disappear soon enough!
> GROUP B: We'll endure, you weaklings! Nothing destroys us, nothing!

Except biology.

> *Quod erat demonstrandum*
> What was to be proven.
> What is proven.

> GROUP A *(laughter)*: Ha ha ha ha ha ha!

III. The Hook and Eye

In part three, discussion gently ebbs away to music. First up, from the top of the charts, the Israeli schlager singer, Daliah Lavi singing her 1970s popular hit, 'Willst du mit mir geh'n?' *Won't you go with me / When my road grows dark? / Won't you go with me / When my night is cold and stark?* Yes, we want to go with her! *When every silence betrays us / What shall we say? / Would a word from you still ease the way?*

During this decade, the work of Walter Benjamin is gradually being rediscovered. He had already suggested a direction for us in the 1920s, asking the question: 'What form would a life take, do you think, that in a crucial moment allowed itself to be determined by the latest popular song?' (Walter Benjamin, *One-way Street and Other Writings.* Tr. J. A. Underwood, Penguin Classics, London 2008).

To answer that question we look at Yiddish lied, not German schlager music. Schlager isn't compatible with rock n' roll, but the Yiddish lied seems both authentic and timely to us. And yet, Yiddish is not easy to understand; it looks like German in transcription (which is why we thought the language would come quickly to us), but it's not German – in reality, it has always been Yiddish, which Franz Kafka made clear long ago. ('Once Yiddish has taken hold of you … then you will no longer understand your earlier tranquility. Then you will feel the true unity of Yiddish so powerfully that you will be afraid, though no longer of Yiddish, but of yourself.' *Essay on the Yiddish Language.* Tr. by David Suchoff, Colby College and Henry Sussman, Yale University). We can't easily speak Yiddish, nor is it easy to understand, and so perhaps it is impossible, perhaps totally incomprehensible to us – so let's turn up the klezmer music, which has no words and is therefore universally understood.

The language of music, that's the language of love!

And this is delightful music to dance to – full of pain and humour, schmerz and vits, a schmerz, a vits, a joke, no, a pain!

It becomes joy! Plus atonement for the crimes of the past! Delightful, 'Ode to Joy,' such joyful-tragic music! *Here we enter, drunk with fire, O Heavenly one, thy shrine*, and we weep with joy for we have found the pain again! From the bottom of our hearts, we thank our dear friends, dear JEWISH friends, our dear murdered JEWISH friends, who we can never know personally because they were murdered and burned in fire, our dear, dear JEWISH dead friends, who should be truly happy, truly, that they are already dead, already dead, otherwise we'd surely love them to death!

Deep inside, so said the poet Hölderlin, one loves the Dead and they are not against it, the Dead, they can't resist the hasty holy water, the Dead, or defend against it, the Dead.

IV. Velcro

In part four, we want to show our love, our great love. Now the rhythm is in our blood. Everyone is clapping and singing, native German speakers along with others – whether or not the others know the language – because as Daliah Lavi sings: '*No language is more than words.*' Moreover, there is concern due to the endless interference of the vehement parailmentarian democrapocratarians, as well as the antivegentellectuals, in particular their aversion to managecapitalistical interblubberllectuals. Listeners from Austria and German-speaking Switzerland will also tune in, and, from now on, we summon every Eurovision nation to the Super-Duper Auschwitz Grand Prix! Millions upon millions are invited from everywhere to take part in this completely open Open Song contest. Make memorials, not concentration camps!

Let the call be heard around the world: Yes, Sarah (or Isaac – forget whatever your real name was), we want to go with you, even if you weep for yesterday! When every silence betrays us, we'll comfort you with our words! Immediately! We're never shutting our traps again.

And now people stream in from all over the world because they can't bear the gaping hole we left in the middle of our city. People present models of their designs to fill the site with boulders and iron beams, or with grand gestures and huge concrete blocks – concrete blocks last longest because concrete never burns! Never burns! Never burns! It never burns. Whoever's made the worst model just rips open his big trap of a mouth a little bit wider, just a bit wider, and out spews talk from his talking hole, his yakking trap, and in no time, the pit will be filled with concrete blocks, rough-paved roads, grand gestures and grandiose words.

Now they want to go with us, they want the fear that time can never heal.

They want to go with us, now that we're no longer here, and you weep for yesteryear.

All of them, every person the whole world over, is united here as one people, and sings together now: the great song, the pretty song, the new song, the best song (c.f. Heinrich Heine, 17th-century German Jewish poet), which goes like this: *We call it love, we call it luck, / No language is more than words.*

Now with the circumstances settled, we can dance again.

> *LET US GO THEN, you and I,*
> *When the evening is spread out against the sky*
> *Like a patient etherized upon a table*
> 'The Love Song of J. Alfred Prufrock,' T. S. Eliot

Since he was looking forward to talking to Graziela later, his walk home was easier than usual.

> *Let us go then, you and I*

Even so, his path led over tiny gold-hued cobblestones engraved with names and placed in front of the homes of the people whose names were on the tiny memorial stones; and beneath the name of each resident, the date of his birth and when and to where he'd been deported and the date of his death, always prior to 1945. The stones were also in front of new houses erected on the site of the ones formerly occupied by people named on the stones; the old buildings having been destroyed in the war, or no longer in existence for another reason. The dates, so familiar, of the residents' deportations and deaths, were never too far apart, and they were always dead before the end of the war. Or missing. The resident or householder. Women and men, children and the elderly. Frambach didn't want to step on the tiny gold-hued headstones. On many stones one could read the names of several people who had belonged together, the whole family deported like cattle.

> *Let us go then, you and I,*
> *When the evening is spread out against the sky*

55

Of course, this evening, as on every other evening, today as on countless days, he walked carefully between the gold-hued memorial stones, gold-hued, teeny tiny stones; careful, careful never to accidently step on these stones; never tread on the name ... deported on ... to Auschwitz, never let street dirt touch the name ... deported on ... to Treblinka, never touch the names ... deported on ... to Theresienstadt. For so long, it had seemed there were a thousand little memorial stones and no world between them; for so long, he'd walked as if the pavement had no regular stones, only those gold-hued headstones. He didn't need to think; his wooden body walked automatically, the caution deep in his bones.

Some stones had gone dark because they'd been there a long time. They looked like real cobblestones, these teeny tiny memorial stones for murdered people; people who had become unique through no accomplishment, about whom nothing was particularly unusual, until their names turned up on a list, a deportation list, and then they became very special, unlike any other people. And the ordinary grey footpath had become his stepping stones over a sea of little memorial stones gold-hued or tarnished – so many, so many little memorial stones, so many, many, many, so many, so many, so many.

He wore his coat like a shield. He hadn't buttoned it up but held it together, his left hand above his heart. With the right hand, he clasped the handle of his ancient, well-worn brown leather briefcase. He bent forward slightly, fixing his gaze on the path between the stones, checking his route. In the blink of an eye, he saw the stones his feet might touch, though they were protected by shoes and socks from making real contact. He placed each foot painstakingly, not to stumble on the many cobblestones, so many stumbling blocks.

'Stumbling Blocks,' the official name of the tiny gold-hued memorial stones, was conceived by an artist as a public art installation. He continues to make and install them; in the meantime, they have become a staple of German cities – like streets, buildings, and sewer systems.

Let us go then, you and I,
When the evening is spread out against the sky
Like a patient etherized upon a table

Evening had already begun. It wouldn't be long now before he talked to Graziela, the only person with whom he ever spoke, who spoke to him, the only one, a golden stepping stone in a grey sea.

After work, go home, return to your place, to yourself. Time to eat. Have dinner. Make tea or drink a glass of water. Sit at the table. Put salami on bread. Or stand at the counter and chop vegetables into bite-sized pieces. Maybe beat two eggs in a little pan, sauté with butter. Listen to the radio. Follow the discussion on the nightly BBC World Service (to which every Tom, Dick, and Harry worldwide contributes an opinion on some highly topical subject). Has the United Nations failed, thereby worsening the terrible situation in Darfur? What's happening to freedom of speech in China? What are Russia's objectives? Has the Cold War resumed? Or maybe don't listen to the radio. Maybe open the window, and during dinner at the kitchen table, listen to children clamour in the garden behind the building. Best to eat slowly, it's healthier. Best to eat slowly because what's happening after dinner? What might you do tonight anyway? There was no way to know when to expect Graziela's call. Don't picture Graziela, who might be making out with Joachim right now – don't picture it. It's too nauseating, and therefore not difficult to imagine something else. But what? If possible, don't think about anything. Empty the dishwasher. Get another cup of tea or glass of water. Go to the desk, turn the computer on, and as you go, switch on the router.

No one had sent an email, of course, who would? For that, he would need to know someone who'd do that. But he doesn't know such a person. There are only newsletters from press offices like the Brandenburg Memorial Foundation, the Heinrich Böll Foundation, the New Society for a Market Economy Initiative, and others who've somehow got hold of his private email. He could unsubscribe from the newsletters, of course, but why?

Then there'd be no email ever. At least this way he had an inkling of what people were busy doing and what they thought was important. What was important to them. An inkling of what others found important. That there were, out there, people for whom things were important.

Now maybe read the paper online. He might also read the articles he'd clipped from the daily paper over the past several months, but they were in the kitchen. It wasn't as if he didn't have time to read each on the day it appeared, his evenings were all equally empty, but he lacked the desire. And yet he felt morally obliged to keep up with political and contemporary affairs, such as: an extensive report on the monetary reform of 1947 and its effect on the country; an examination of the disjuncture between the Quran, Western liberal civil law, and the practice of secular law in general; a description of the artwork owned by Jews in Germany in the 1930s, sold under duress for less than the art was worth, a transaction the owners' descendants now wanted to have reversed or, at least, to have their losses acknowledged. For professional reasons, he needed to read that one. They were all in the kitchen.

The children would play outside until they couldn't any longer, but already their clamour was softer, light fading, night gathering round.

He switched on his desk lamp so as not to strain his eyes, which could happen if the only light came from his computer screen.

Again, he sat at a computer, as always, at a computer: window of the world, windows on the world – what exactly had been the name of that restaurant in the World Trade Center?

He could instantly search for it, the computer was on, connected to the Internet.

He put 'Schanghai' in the search engine and 'about 320,000' hits came up at once. Then he typed in English, 'Shanghai.' That called up 'about 86,500,000' hits to the pit of his stomach, and he felt a swell inside, a surge of heavy depression that he swallowed by clicking away from the browser. Once more he sat looking at the empty monitor, dark blue, *colour of the introvert* ('Fragments,' Gottfried Benn, 1950).

The Internet connection remained constant. And continuous.

Only time fades with every second, tick tick tock, until we die, already another second gone by.

HE DECIDED IN FAVOUR OF HIS MADAM CHANCELLOR, whose weekly podcast was available on the Internet, and who had often helped him kill time pleasantly, killing the evening until bedtime. She had saved him from himself so often, from the burden of time, this singular woman whose name was divisible by three, for whom he hadn't voted – for which he was sorry. Now he saw how steadfast she was in her role – the official title of her position was Bundeskanzlerin and could be divided perfectly by three, thereby making five! – how staunchly she pursued her aims, did and said what she thought right (maybe, even, when it wasn't), so that she had grown dear to him; for the first time in his life, he found himself in agreement with the governing regime (gov-ern-ing reg-ime), and wished with all his heart that her election results had been better – the latest were her party's worst. She worked hard and thought that effort was crucial: 'I expect a government about which people will say: they make an effort despite their different opinions on issues, seeking solutions to our problems for all our benefit.' She'd said this at the press conference held before the German parliament's summer recess. Now he watched it from beginning to end, a full ninety minutes, as long as an average film, and felt she had never lied, and understood why Helmut Kohl had called her 'my girl'. If he were Helmut Kohl, he would have called her that too. She wore a red jacket. He thought someone had probably once told her that football teams wearing red shirts won more often. Winners wear red. Frambach wore muted colours, never red. But he wasn't a politician and, anyway, he never thought much about those categories – winners and losers. For him, it was enough to make it through, *to endure is everything* ('Requiem for Wolf Graf von Kalckreuth', Rainer Maria Rilke).

At the end of the press conference, she had thanked the moderator nicely, bidding farewell to the journalists, 'Have a wonderful summer.' She was so polite.

Unfortunately, she'd sat throughout the conference with her hands hidden beneath a wooden desk. Her hands were what fascinated him most about her. During her weekly address, her hands were often, though not always, visible. She spoke with the fingertips of her hands pressed together, and if they separated (rarely), they would immediately dart back to meet at the tips as if bound by rubber bands. He'd once tried to copy her and understood how difficult it was. His fingertips would not meet; more often, his hands bustled around independent of each other, stabbing air. But Angela Merkel made it seem effortless, drawing a circle of concentration around herself with her fingers, hands and arms, probably a protective fence. She also parted her hands to emphasise important words: DEMOCRACY, EUROPE, OUR COUNTRY, WE SHALL, I WOULD LIKE. Sometimes she pursed together the fingertips of her right hand as if she were striking a drum with her knuckles, and with this gesture emphasised a single word: FAIR wages, INDEPENDENT achievement, I EXPECT. And sometimes she separated her hands with two or three backward jerks for a little emphasis: the FEDERAL REPUBLIC of Germany, ONE example. Her hands were unlike anyone else's, entirely her own, and they underscored their service to the greater good. As the state's second highest official, she expended such concern and effort, whereas her fingertips met effortlessly again and again, as if there were no other place for them, as if her hands ran on train tracks back and forth, apart and together, like little carriages. They must stay coupled otherwise the train would break apart or there'd be no train. Otherwise you couldn't chug into the future with these words, these words that were not *lightning* and would not *disturb the world's sleep* (cf. 'Er rührte an den Schlaf der Welt (Lenin)'. Johannes R. Becher and Hanns Eisler, 1949). These were soothing words. Dear Fatherland.

AND WITH THAT IT WAS TEN O'CLOCK and he was almost tired enough to sleep, but he had to wait for a call.

He still had all his LPs from before there were CDs, from when he was interested in popular music, back when it was normal to follow popular music and he and his contemporaries were known as the 'No Future Generation' – in hindsight, an accurate moniker. Maybe that's why he'd wandered into history. Whatever. Now he was old enough to refer objectively to his youth as 'the past' and to call people who were the age he'd been then 'young people' and to think they were weird.

It didn't take him long to find 'Amok/Koma' by Abwärts (recorded in August 1980. Zickzack-Platten. ZZ10); he didn't have very many records and hadn't bought one in twenty years. After turning the volume button a hair beyond the mark where nothing came out of the speakers, he listened to exactly one song, the fourth on side one, which lasted two minutes and forty-five seconds.

Polly, it costs more than one woman to change my name into
shanghai
stinker
sailor, your home is the sea
your friends are the stars
above rio and shanghai
above bali and hawaii
if I were a sailor
and didn't know where I was
where would I be then?
where would I be then?
above rio and shanghai?

63

above bali and hawaii?
above rio and shanghai?
above bali and hawaii?

He lifted the needle again, gingerly took the record from the player, and slid it into its sleeve and its place. Next, he took the record beside it ('recorded december 80 – january 81 in conny's studio.' Virgin Records 203 644-320) and listened for three minutes and fifty-four seconds to the second track on side one, called 'the mussolini', which was the very best song the band Deutsch-Amerikanische Freundschaft ever recorded, a stroke of brilliance the rest of the album didn't live up to. The two men (the whole band) never appreciated they had a masterpiece with this track. Not only was the music the most interesting, the lyrics were even better, asking you to dance 'the adolf hitler', 'the jesus christ', 'the communism', one after another, perfectly capturing the punk spirit of the times.

That spirit had brought the word 'zeitgeist' back into fashion. They spoke of the zeitgeist they lived in – suddenly aware of themselves and surprised at their importance; in all likelihood, they were more important than Mussolini, Adolf Hitler, Jesus Christ or Communism, at least to themselves.

Then he listened to the track once again.

Between calls for various 'dances' came an urgent demand, 'I want to hold your hand,' which sent a shiver of tenderness through him that brought tears to his eyes. This demand, he knew, was perhaps first a plea, *I want to hold your hand*, and it had stirred him deeply back when the music was popular and the lyrics had been discussed and labelled fascistic, *I want to hold your hand*; but that was in the past when he hadn't known how human the need was to reach for someone's hand – particularly in light of a world in which one's beliefs had become irrelevant and one realised abruptly how alone each person was, eddying into himself, here and everywhere, now and forever.

I want to hold your hand.

At the date the music was recorded, he recognised, he'd just become an adult, could barely vote, and still had half a year before finishing high school.

He returned the record to its place with the others.

He turned off the stereo.

He turned back to the phone. In the time he'd found the two records and listened to both songs, a full twenty minutes of his life had been taken from the future and turned into the past.

He sat by the phone, waited until ten forty-five, then called Graziela.

After the fifth ring she picked up, saying only 'Yes?'

'You were going to call me.'

'I will,' she said, 'but I can't talk now,' and hung up.

HE TOOK A PIECE OF PAPER AND WROTE: 'In complete surrender, I lay my head under night's slaughtering axe.'

Then he sat at his desk by the phone, the fountain pen in his hand, and did nothing.

Around eleven-thirty he went to the kitchen for a glass of water.

After that he sat at his desk again, looking at the sentence he'd written that wasn't his.

With great precision, he filled the rest of the paper with drawings of boxes, some filled in, some not; the kind of doodle that kept you concentrated during a phone call. But he wasn't on a call, he was just waiting for one.

As the last hour of the day struck, he switched on the radio to listen to the news, or so he thought, just as earlier he'd thought he'd watched the programme out of support for his country, though, in reality, he'd wanted to see his Chancellor; and now, really, he just wanted to hear German Broadcasting bid goodnight with one of the national anthems. Played by a small string ensemble, it was intimate. A German listener would expect nothing more. Having watched his Chancellor endeavour to be a good leader for so much of the evening, he was now overcome with emotion, as he sometimes was, and wanted to weep – if only he were able – for all the people who took such pains, always trying to do the right thing. The Chancellor had taken the time to show the people a common touch, and the radio bid each citizen goodnight with Brecht's 'Children's Hymn,' in a manner guaranteed to be humble. There was nothing grand, no pathos, nothing overwhelming, just an urgent desire for harmony.

> *And because we'll make it better*
> *Let us guard and love our home.*
> *Love it as our dearest country*
> *As the others love their own.*

Exactly. Surely that's what we've done,

> *That the people give up flinching*
> *At the crimes which we evoke*

when we hold out our hands. And so we offer them our dear little, chubby little hands.

Back in those days, he hadn't consciously chosen to dance the Adolf Hitler, it just happened. Most likely, he hadn't thought about it. *No future.* He couldn't remember if he'd ever considered another path for his life. *Only the past.* He hadn't thought about it and so there hadn't been anything else.

He wanted to hold someone's hand.

WHEN THE PHONE RANG, HE DIDN'T KNOW WHERE HE WAS, but he knew he was dead. Although his ears and head functioned, his body wouldn't move at all. He had nothing but fear in his head – his brain stuck in a paralysed body.

The ringing came down from Elysian heights,
down from the peaks, with thin, clear Alpine air
to where he lay with the worms in earth's heavy, damp guts.

Slowly he grasped that he'd been in a deep sleep, and with one arm (on which hung a thousand pounds of sleep), he lifted the quilt with a tremendous exertion of will. At once he was ice cold. Summoning even more titanic power, he pulled his feet from the bed, balanced himself, and stood. He staggered to his desk where the phone was ringing on and on, and finally put the receiver to his ear as he stood barefoot and cold:

'Yes?'

'Have I woken you?' asked Graziela.

'Yes.'

'Oh, I'm so sorry, but I promised to call.'

'Yes, what time is it now?'

'I'm not sure, wait,' Graziela searched for the time, 'two.'

'I was in the first deep sleep phase, I guess,' he said. His teeth chattered and a shiver swept over him.

'Go and put something on,' ordered Graziela, 'I'll wait,' and he obeyed. Still, he was cold sitting there, and grew still colder when he heard that Joachim and his wife were separating. There was a lot to discuss, explained Graziela. That's why she couldn't call earlier.

This is the end, he thought. If Graziela and Joachim began a normal relationship, there would be no place for him.

All at once, he felt deceived. It should have been everlasting: Joachim responsible for Graziela's love life, Hans the shoulder she cried on.

Although he loathed Joachim, he had kept Hans from worrying that his and Graziela's friendship might change – which was exactly what he feared because he knew she'd been miserable without a love life. Even though they'd never discussed it explicitly. That had been the best thing about their bond, their relationship, their friendship – oh no, he was already thinking in the past tense.

They had never really spoken about their own personal misery, only about their common German history and how it made them feel. Later about the happiness, if you could call it that, which Joachim brought Graziela.

He was silent.

Naturally, she had got on his nerves.

'Hans?'

But when people saw each other often, it was to be expected. Or, rather, when they talked so often.

'Are you still there?' Graziela said.

They didn't meet very often. But they telephoned daily, mostly more than once a day. That was the certainty they shared! That they could speak to each other at any time of the day, even at two in the morning, for example!

'Say something,' said Graziela. 'What's the matter?'

'I ...'

'Yes?'

'I ... I'm only wondering ...'

'What then?'

now what will become of me, he thought,

'Why this is happening,' he said. 'You told me clearly that it was unlikely that an adulterer would separate from his or her spouse if the extramarital relationship continued for longer than one year; and that if the adulterous affair has not become a publicly acknowledged conventional relationship within the first year, it would never become one, which means that the adulterous affair must alter within the first year or will remain unchanged – and yet your affair has been continuing for four years now.'

'Why are you talking like that?' Graziela said.

'This is how I talk,' he said. I always talk like a lawyer when I'm upset, he thought, she must know that. 'I just don't get it.'

Then there was silence. He heard Graziela breathe, and he closed his eyes, sensing his feet had become blocks of ice, and waited for Graziela to begin weeping.

'It isn't Joachim who wants to separate,' she said finally. 'His wife wants to separate from him.'

At that he forced not only his eyes but his whole face to shut, and pressed his cold feet into the floor, to get what he'd heard out of the world. She was breathing very loudly. He breathed heavily, too, because he wanted to do something he almost never did – he wanted to say what he thought. He not only thought but also said:

'You don't deserve that,' and then he heard Graziela crying.

Joachim's wife knew nothing about her; in fact, the wife had fallen in love with someone else, Graziela explained, sobbing. And Joachim hadn't yet told his wife about her; in fact, he'd said to her that he didn't want to make the situation any more complicated than it already was.

'But it would make the situation much simpler.'

'Yes,' she sobbed, 'that's what I said, too.'

'And?'

'And – nothing.' Again, she sobbed.

Coward, he thought. Henpecked. Jerk. What an asshole. And once more he said what he thought:

'Coward.'

'Yes, that's what I thought,' and then Graziela couldn't speak another word because she was sobbing so pitifully; and throughout it he wished she'd stop blubbering.

'I'm going to Shanghai,' he said. That did it. After a quick sniffle, she spoke normally.

'To Shanghai? How did that happen? What will you do in Shanghai?'

'Oh, what else? Examine some small estate and procure it for our archive – it belongs to some emigrant popular music composer, schlager or something – anyway, um, crates of his stuff were like in a corner or attic – I don't know actually if they have, um, attics in Shanghai – anyway, when the house was vacated – to build, like, a skyscraper – they found packing crates. As usual, Marschner was first to get his fat paws on them.'

'Why are you talking like that?' she said again. 'You sound totally stressed out.'

'I am,' he said, 'I'm totally stressed.'

'But why?' shouted Graziela. 'It's great! You're going to Shanghai!'

Yes, great, he thought,

'Yes, great,' he said,

maybe, he thought, if there were something (som-eth-ing) going on here that I was saying goodbye to, or better put, if I were saying goodbye to someone (any-one), and if I were coming back to someone (any-one),

'Twelve hours on a plane, not a word of Chinese, then hustle with some know-nothing museum jerks ...'

'Oh, Hans,' interrupted Graziela, sounding dangerously close to tears again, 'I really don't know what's wrong with you.

Oh, he thought, I don't know what's wrong with me either.

'You're so hostile these days, so self-involved, so ... I don't know.'

Great, he thought, now this.

'And you're always so "Joachim this, Joachim that" ...' he said in another act of self-defence – a successful one, because Graziela began to sob. And he was ashamed of himself.

'I'm so sorry. I'm sorry. Please ...'

'Never mind,' she said, sniffling. The weeping stopped. Started again. 'Never mind, never mind.' Stopped again.

'I'm really sorry,' he said once more, but she'd already stopped crying.

'We'll see each other on Friday. We can talk then. About Shanghai. About Joachim.'

About us, he thought.

'Yes.' He uttered the tiniest sound.

'Good night,' she said, 'sleep well.' In reality, she was such a good miserable person. He was even more ashamed of himself.

'Good night.'

'Good night,' she said once more, then the line clicked.

He put the phone down carefully, so it made no sound. Very gently. And sat for a while at his desk, hands on the flat surface, and hung his head; his cold feet were a fitting punishment for his heartlessness.

Loneliness had eaten at him for so long, maybe now it was devouring him. Maybe nothing remained of him but pieces of equipment piled together. A talking-machine and thinking-machine no longer in sync; a walking-machine that took him to work and home, and put him to bed; a metabolic apparatus, human junk, that's what he'd become, functionally alive. And the machines were jumbled together with no aesthetic sense or intelligence. With no reason to exist.

THAT NIGHT HE HAD A TERRIBLE NIGHTMARE. In the dream, Frau Kermer laughed often and very loudly. Her face became a shrieking mask, her ever-motionless hair shading her features like a shiny hood, and she was Joachim's wife. Joachim lay at her feet, trying to grab her ankles, but she kept pedalling her legs like someone treading water. Again and again, he reached for her ankles, until finally she put her foot on his head, laughing so gruesomely her face turned green and blue. Marschner stood near her, also laughing, and shook his Medusa head of carousel chains. One of the flying seats hit Graziela, who was kneeling nearby dressed in a flowing blue robe, her long hair loose, and begging with her hands pressed together. When Marschner's carousel seat hit her, blood poured down her temple in a wide stream and she fell sideways to the floor. Frambach tried to reach out to her but couldn't move. Suddenly, Marschner and Frau Kermer appeared in front of him like a stockade fence, pressed together so tightly that a piece of paper couldn't have slid between them. Frau Kermer's face had returned to its normal colour, and as the two took a step forwards, she stepped on Joachim's head. Frambach heard the painful grinding and then Joachim's head was unrecognisable; it looked like a heap of fat, squirming worms. Frau Kermer and Marschner aimed their laughter at him, yet there was no sound. At the same time, it was loud, unbearably so, as loud as the grinding of the world's gears. When he tried to escape, he saw a slick black wall behind him, looming toward the sky. However, he saw nothing in the sky because it was pitch dark, and as he backed up against this rear wall, the wall turned into concentration camp prisoners. Their emaciated bodies were piled to the sky, wrapped in tattered rags, and they were alive. Arms of skin and bone reached from behind, and Frau Kermer's and Marschner's hands stretched out in front, also reaching for him, but their hands were large and fleshy. Behind him he saw Wolkenkraut standing beside his parents, and next to him, his wife and daughter, who held a small Chinese flag in her hand; and farther behind them were many thin arms that flung themselves over Frambach's shoulders, his back, his hips, holding onto his legs tightly, and just as the large, fat hands reached out in front and were about to touch him, he woke at last.

His heart raced. He opened his eyes wide but couldn't see a thing – it was still night, his heart raced. Then he noticed the outline of his closet and the window behind the drapes. Although it was night, it was never completely dark in the middle of the city where he lived, never as pitch dark as in his dream. His heart sped on, and he didn't know how to catch his breath. He didn't want to let the air out of his lungs, but it needed to escape. He sucked in again at once, as deeply as before, and didn't want to let go. His heart raced. The alarm clock read five in the morning – the best time for a police raid - but no one was at his door. In the dark, he went to the toilet, where the small green light of his electric toothbrush shone out. Then he lay down in the exact centre of his bed, his hands on his solar plexus, and forced himself not to squeeze his eyes shut but to let them close gently, and he willed his breath in and out.

He fell again into a deep sleep and woke feeling exhausted when the alarm rang at the chosen hour.

THE LEFTIST DEMONSTRATOR, WHO CLAIMS he fought with the PLO against Israel, was captured by the Israelis, thrown into prison and then freed in an Arab-Israeli prisoner exchange, now asserts that the Israelis should leave the country. Asked the question of where they should go, back to Poland perhaps? he SHOUTS, yes, definitely, back to Poland!

The hijacking of Air France Flight 139 to Entebbe in the summer of 1976: a German woman stands on the runway re-enacting the selection at Auschwitz, separating the hostages into Jews and non-Jews, and letting the non-Jews go free.

The sign in the health-food store states: No Fruit or Vegetables Grown in Israel Sold Here.

The man born in the late 1930s who studies Flavius Josephus' *History of Jewish War* argues that the reason the Jews have suffered so much misery is due to their obstinacy.

The proposal to rename Potsdamer Platz, Berlin's central square, 'Judenplatz' so that people must think about 'it' is discussed zealously, and yet no one points out that Potsdamer Platz would have to be renamed 'Auschwitz Platz' to achieve this goal.

Zog nit keyn mol, az du geyst dem letstn veg.

The director of a concentration camp memorial asks if anyone has seen their exhibition's latest installation from the Netherlands about a former Dutch prisoner who was amazing, better even than Primo Levi.

The woman, a representative from one of the retributive justice institutions, brims with enthusiasm about the elderly people she has recently met at the conference of the International Auschwitz Committee in Auschwitz; truly the crème de la crème of survivors, she says, they have all written books.

GRAZIELA CALLED THE NEXT MORNING as he retrieved his coat from the rack in the Bureau's reception foyer.

'Good morning, Frau Schönbluhm,' he heard Frau Kermer say behind him. He turned around, holding his coat as tenderly as a beloved. As Frau Kermer pressed her hand over the mouthpiece, he saw how very narrow and long-fingered her hand was in reality; she stared hard at him, her eyebrows raised in question. Understanding that she wanted to know if she should get rid of Graziela, he felt a surge of hate through his body that left him speechless. He pulled his coat on securely, bandaging his pain, and nodded towards his office. He walked fast, almost racing to the phone, not stopping to hang up his coat; in fact, he lay it like a blanket over himself.

'Graziela,' he said, 'my love,' as if he'd now reached dry land, safe once more, 'how did you sleep last night?'

She began wailing right away.

'I slept terribly, too,' he said.

She sobbed.

'Now I'm dragging you into it! I don't want to!'

'It's really okay.' He heard her blow her nose.

'Are you still there?' she asked.

'Yes,' he said, and thought, of course, I'm always here, 'of course, I'm here.'

'He betrayed me. He didn't give it a second thought, he betrayed me on the spot. He's a pig. He did it right off, didn't consider not betraying me for a second. Obviously I mean absolutely nothing to him. Nothing at all. I couldn't sleep all night, I was so furious.'

'Fury is good once in a while.'

'You think? I don't know.'

'Hell hath no fury ...' he recited.

'So they say.'

'It makes it easier to remember.'

'Oh ...' she sighed and began to wail. 'I thought it was love,' she sobbed. He closed his eyes. 'I thought ...'

She couldn't speak any more and sobbed. He slid deeper into his chair, drawing his coat up to cover himself. Saf-ety. Ref-uge.

'Maybe you were mistaken,' he said, immediately wishing he hadn't. Wro-ng m-ove. Hea-rta-che. No wonder she couldn't stop weeping.

He was ashamed and thought he would have to bear it.

He crawled deeper under his coat.

He heard a knock at the door.

'No!' he called.

'No what?' said Graziela, interrupting her sobs.

'I wasn't speaking to you,' he said. 'Someone knocked at the door.'

'Now I've bothered you at work again!' began Graziela, sobbing, while the door opened, offering him a glimpse of Frau Kermer posing as if Helmut Newton were about to take her picture. Now it was his turn to put his hand over the mouthpiece; he hissed: 'Not now! You can see I'm on the telephone,' and the door closed.

'I really don't mean to .... I don't want to bother you at work.'

'You aren't bothering me.'

'Oh, but,' she countered.

'But what?'

'I just want to hear how your night was.'

'You already know how it was.'

'Yes,' now she wasn't crying, 'and I want to thank you.'

'For what?'

'For everything,' she said very seriously.

It was quiet for a few moments.

'Thank you,' he said finally, and then, 'What about the organ concert?'

'We'll go,' she said, 'it's not for three days.'

'Good. Call me whenever you want. Okay?'

'Yes, I will' she said, 'I do that anyway. What else would I do?'

That's true, he thought.

'Call me, too, whenever you want,' she said. 'I'm so sorry I woke you up last night.'

'Don't worry.'

'Thanks,' she said. 'I don't know what I'd do without you.'

'Likewise,' he said.

'See you soon.'

'Bye now.' (Bye-bye now).

He hung his coat on the hook near the door, his briefcase holding the coat's hem in place. With his hand on his coat, he stood quietly for a moment. He took a deep breath, opened the door, and propelled by hate, walked as quickly and firmly as earlier – but in the opposite direction – towards the reception area. Hate seethed all the way to his toes, his nerves strung to the highest pitch. He imagined he would butcher Frau Kermer so she would never say another word, that he would descend upon her with hurricane force, tell her what he thought of her, all of it! Namely, that she was an exceptionally unbearable person, a soul-exterminating machine in human form – all told, a stupid cow! He would say it, but then he wondered how; he didn't know the right curse words. Should he simply say she was a piece of shit who would have brought joy to Adolf Eichmann?

Storming along the dark hall, he stopped precisely at the reception desk as if the floor were marked. He stood very straight in front of her and breathed deeply, inhaling and exhaling.

And despite his great loathing for her, he couldn't do more than inhale and exhale.

If he insulted her, which she deserved, he would be fraternising with her, and that he would not do. He wouldn't lower himself to her level. He was furious. It made his blood boil. To think she'd suggested they gang up against Graziela, who was so infinitely better a person than she was. That stupid cow, the stu-pid stu-pid cow.

She glanced up without emotion from under her motionless blonde hair. He concentrated on her so as not to look away first, to stare her down. He held his hate against her cold, and knew his hate was stronger when she looked away first; she disguised it as work-related by looking at her computer screen, the content of which he was unable to read. Armed with her ballpoint pen, she pointed nonchalantly at the screen as she looked over to him, saying:

'I'm booking your flight to Shanghai right now. I wanted to know your preferences. In any case I've been instructed to book the least expensive flight. KLM is cheapest.'

'KLM flies via Amsterdam,' he said at once, mirroring her chilly, business-like tone, 'which is in the other direction.' His quick-witted reply stoked his courage.

She paused momentarily to give her contempt adequate space. Then she said:

'All the flights go via airports that are in "other" directions. It appears you would like to fly Aeroflot.'

Now he would land his point.

'There are other airports besides Moscow that are in the right direction. For example, Helsinki.'

'Helsinki?!' She snorted. 'Helsinki is north of here. That's also in the other direction.' She smiled patronisingly at him. What was more, as she smiled, he saw every paper-thin, scraggly tooth in her mouth. Such ugly teeth. How embarrassing to bare such ridiculously ugly teeth. He soared high, feeling not an iota of doubt; he had a beautiful set of teeth, which he wouldn't abuse by snarling at her.

'Frau Kermer,' he said, articulating carefully, 'you should not make a fool of yourself by displaying your inadequate knowledge of geography.' He became still colder and spoke ever more precisely. 'Helsinki is indeed north of here and yet also far to the east, and if you consider that the earth is a sphere, and, in addition, that the flight path to East Asia goes over Siberia, you will easily see why Finnair, registered in Helsinki, advertises the shortest route to East Asia.'

Now her face was lacquered with pure hate.

'Therefore, you will book the Finnair flight or nothing,' he said, 'and you will not purchase the cheapest seat, you will book one in Business Class.'

'I'm not allowed,' she said quickly.

'Cattle cars.'

'Excuse me?' she said. It sounded like a rebuke.

'Cattle cars,' he repeated. 'Eleven seats to a row, squeezed between strangers, unable to move, sitting for twelve hours, filthy bathrooms. Animal transport.'

He cleared his throat before continuing:

'Pardon me. Of course, I meant people transported by cattle car. Auschwitz. I think you, too, will have heard of it. Treblinka. Sobibor. These are names with which you must be acquainted. Theresienstadt. Riga. Cattle cars. I will fly Business Class.'

It was like a dream. He'd said everything he thought, and it was all correct.

He was jubilant. He smiled without forcing himself, because it came from the heart. But it was only a thin smile; he was careful not to show her how happy he was.

'Under no circumstance,' said Frau Kermer, who felt she was completely on the right side of things. 'I have been instructed to be as frugal as possible when managing our business expenses. After all, we are responsible to the federal government and to our sponsors for our expense accounts.'

'In our ministry and among our sponsors,' he countered, patiently pronouncing every syllable, which was easy with these words and felt so good that he started over: 'In our ministry and among our sponsors, there is no one who would spend twelve hours travelling for work in a cattle car. I will fly Business Class. And, moreover, you will book me into a five-star hotel.'

'Herr Frambach' said Frau Kermer, who now attempted to pronounce every syllable of each word just as he had, but it wasn't as easy given what she had to say. 'Herr Frambach,' she repeated, 'your insistence puts me in a difficult situation.' She was coated in a layer of ice. Her hair gleamed dangerously. It's only sugar frosting, he thought; in reality, the icing on the bitch is just frosting.

He felt no fear.

'Business Class. Five-star hotel,' he repeated. 'It must be fit for a human being. It must be.'

Over her face lay a craquelure mask. Hate poured from the fissures.

He held her gaze.

She lost once again.

'You will have to speak to Herr Marschner about this,' she said at last, 'I won't be responsible.'

'You, Frau Kermer,' and this was the final triumph, 'are definitely not responsible. You are not authorised for this responsibility. Make an appointment for me with Herr Marschner, and I will gladly speak for myself.'

With that, he turned his back to her, and returned to his office with measured steps.

He was filled with happiness until he left the reception room. In the corridor, unhappiness weighed him down again.

The flight from Helsinki to Shanghai was actually only nine hours, not twelve. He'd exaggerated there. Even counting the flight to Helsinki, a flight of merely two hours, the trip wasn't twelve hours; altogether, pure flight time would be eleven hours. Exactly as Finnair advertised. Plus waiting time in transit at Helsinki airport, of course, but no one was buckled into a seat during that time. Also, an airbus didn't seat eleven people in a row, only eight, four in the middle, two on either side, which meant he'd really exaggerated; Marschner would use this argument against him and his need for a Business Class seat. He'd grossly exaggerated; in essence, he'd lied. In the end, he'd fly Economy. He hadn't won, the whole thing was not his triumph but hers. A great triumph for her, a crushing defeat for him.

He was not cut out for this war.

He was already beaten as his office door shut behind him.

He turned on the computer, looked at the programs on his screen and was unable to move, he couldn't even input his username or password.

At last he lifted the phone and called Graziela. He said nothing about his triumph or happiness or that he'd had a moment of inspiration; instead, he said that he'd lied and was afraid of ending up a fool. There was a chance, too, that he'd be fired soon, since lying was probably adequate grounds for dismissal. Graziela couldn't make sense of it and asked him to narrate the events in order. She asked objective questions, which he could answer objectively.

Exactly what had happened? What did she say? What did you say? What did she say after that? What did you answer? And how do you know that Finnair has the fastest flight to Asia?

'Everyone knows that.'

'I didn't know that.'

You don't spend your evenings on the Internet, reading every piece of crap, he thought.

'Well, now you know,' he said.

'I can't deal with your tone right now.'

This again.

She didn't sound as if she was about to cry; it was worse.

Of course, she was right.

He was being inconsiderate.

He excused himself and explained how it was that he knew that sort of thing.

They said goodbye.

He rested his hands in his lap and hung his head.

He didn't want to log into the archive.

His screen, on standby, was black.

He saw it as he opened his eyes again and lifted his head.

After a while he was able to raise his hand to the portfolio with the not-yet-archived papers from Wolkenkraut. He opened it and read the document on top: 'Account of my time in several concentration camps.' That finished him off.

He closed the portfolio and lowered his head; now he could have laid it under a guillotine. For a long time, he remained in this position. He was ready to be executed.

The stretch was good for his neck and back.

MICHAEL THEUNISSEN, *EARLY SKETCHES OF MODERNITY*. Ancient Melancholy and Medieval Acedia. Berlin, New York: Walter de Gruyter 1996:

Excerpting Aristotle on Theophrastus:

> *12: Melancholiacs are, first of all, inconsistent with others; second, they are inconsistent with themselves; and third, the black bile from which they receive their name,* mélaina cholé, *is inconsistent. (954b4–10).*

> *13: The internal inconsistency of the melancholiac is reflected in the inconsistency of the melancholia-inducing substance. Ultimately, this concerns a division within the people themselves and within the substrate of their melancholia.*

On Thomas Aquinas: De acedia

> *26f: The name, a Latinised version of the Greek word* akédia, *already indicates something negative:* a-kédia *is a negation of* kēdos, *'care.' The lack of care evoked by the name is not the state of being carefree, as Jesus advocates, but rather a state in which not caring about something one ought to care for leads to unwanted consequences. The burden one sought to avoid returns as a form of tribulation. [Thomas] describes [acedia's] characteristic sadness ... as a heavy sadness, which saps all joy from spiritual work [27] and leads to complete helplessness. ... Acedia is generally understood as tedium. ... Acedia expresses itself through* taedium, *a reluctance that*

can turn into deep repugnance and often ends in torpor, *a state of inertia that devolves into dullness.27: Unlike acedia, melancholia is ... internally divided, without external antithesis. In contrast, acedia is only recognisable as itself when considered alongside joy, which it excludes.*

28f:*Since acedia means losing the ability to rejoice in God, it can be understood as a negative experience of the divine. ... Acedia discloses reality in a particular way. ... One's own existence is felt to be burdensome because of the burden of being. To the sufferer of acedia, the original burden is God laying claim upon him. The pressure to exist in the world intensifies this burden, but the world also veils itself in the illusion that it can replace burdens with desire. Heidegger erased God from this equation and shifted the burden onto the world.*

32: *Acedia is not a sin of action; it is a sin of the heart, the 'heaviness at heart,' which Benjamin discusses in his seventh thesis on the concept of history. But this heaviness results from a reckless separation of the self from the source of joy. Those overcome by acedia have therefore made themselves torpid. ... The doctrine of sin identifies acedia as an act of freedom. This must ... be accepted without reservation. The freedom of acedia is an independent complement to melancholia; a freedom which precedes every act of freedom since it stems from a natural predisposition.*

36: *Thomas understands* a-cedere, *the flight from God, as a process that encompasses the entire dynamic of acedia. He believes that this flight is not passive, but instead a dramatic breakaway. In the final moment, reason yields to horror, revulsion, and the desire to flee from divine goodness;* in fugam et horrorem et detestationem boni divini *(a.3, resp.). Nothing is left for the drama's second act except com-*

plete stasis, a 'forbidden' rest betrayed by the symptoms of in-
ertia and dullness. Acedia's secondary emphasis is therefore
stasis, a middle stage in which everything becomes petrified.

Roland Barthes, *How to Live Together.* Translated by Kate Briggs.
[Comment vivre ensemble] (Lecture course at the Collège de
France 1976–1977.) New York: Columbia University Press 2013.

65: Acedia is the mourning of investment itself, not the thing in-
vested in. In reality, disinvestment in the loved object: can be
a liberation (at last, free of distress!), but can also be a source
of distress: the misery of not being loved. Acedia: what's
mourned is not the image, it's the imaginary. It's what's most
painful: you experience all of the pain and yet are deprived of
the secondary gain that is playing it up for effect.

IN THE AFTERNOON, GRAZIELA HAD TO CHANGE THEIR EVEN-ING PLANS because the music school teachers had called a general meeting at short notice to discuss how to deal with the latest regulations pertaining to independent contractors – meaning not how to adhere to the new rules, but how to circumvent them. The music school was their sole employer, and all were incorporated into the school's curricular schedule; therefore, the government considered them full-time employees. Unfortunately, the new governmental regulations meant the music school would have to pay the employees social security and health insurance benefits, which it could not afford, meaning the teachers would theoreti-cally lose their jobs immediately. The regulations governing the employment of freelance workers had been in effect for ten years, causing agitation and making them continually prove they were independent contractors, not employees, not fraudulent, and this had siphoned off much of the pleasure of daily life. Even the Social Democrats, who wanted everyone to be a civil servant, couldn't figure out a way to make independent contractors into full-time employees without bankrupting the school. The usual.

Graziela took less than half a minute to recount this, since she'd explained it all to him before. She would have to attend the meeting, she said, through to the end. She didn't know exactly when she'd get to the church for the six little organ concerts, one after another, but they agreed she would drive there as soon as her meeting ended and take him home later.

So he made his way alone to the Church of Atonement near Plötzensee, in a housing development built between 1955 and 1961, which, in the spirit of those times, *arose from the ruins and was devoted to the future.*

THE STREETS DON'T ENTER THE HOUSING ESTATE DIRECTLY, instead wending around the eight-storey buildings; strangers won't find the entrance to the complex easily. Each building stands on its own, circled by a meagre green patch that can't conceal the bleakness.

The U-Bahn station, Halemweg, has yellow tiled walls. Teenagers hang out in the exits, which look like assembly halls. Adjacent is a pub, 'Gaststätte im Zentrum', and through its open door there's a view of modest-sized chandeliers and a slot machine to the rear. The pub looks like it hasn't changed since opening day and isn't for young people – it's for those who've grown old with the development. The smell of the deep fryer wafts out the door, accompanying visitors to the next corner where the church's six tall, white concrete walls meet. The church has no windows except for a glass frieze at the top. Only giants could see into these windows, and the dear Lord, of course.

Although the church is located on a main road, to enter it visitors have to walk around the corner and through a court-yard with a tower on one side and the church on the other. In other words, the visitor spirals along a path that winds away from the ugly world, via an inhospitable train station, past an uninviting pub, away from the clean poverty of the petit bourgeoisie.

At last the visitor stands in a small square: to the left, the church, to the right, the parish hall. A wall joins the two, leading from the church's vestibule to the square. Inscribed on the wall, from left to right, are the words 'Golgotha Plötzensee Auschwitz Hiroshima Walls.' The words may also be read right to left, from outside to inside, from the sorry world to the Protestant Church's paltry lap. Then they would read: 'Walls Hiroshima Auschwitz Plötzensee Golgotha,' and be no more agreeable.

In front of this wall, there's more concrete, and a boulder with these words (Genesis 4:10):

> *Listen*
> *the blood of your brother*
> *cries out to me*
> *from the ground*

The words are made out of nails.

HE ARRIVED ON TIME, meaning he was overly punctual. Much too early. The usual.

People had gathered in the church's glassed-in porch, undoubtedly regulars; they seemed familiar with the territory. To them, the church was welcoming.

Behind a folding table, two older women in pastel puffer jackets stood in front of the word 'Golgotha'. On the table, drinks were offered, and bread rolls, already cut in half for the congregation to make their own sliced cheese sandwiches. There was coffee in a massive cylindrical metal container and herbal teabags near a large thermos of hot water, as well as mineral water and two kinds of bottled fruit juice, and red wine in a box shaped like a cask. It had a plastic tap that extended beyond the table's edge to easily accommodate a plastic cup beneath it.

The crowd of younger people all wore jeans and faded sweatshirts. A young woman sporting a greasy blonde ponytail was flirting with the only handsome young man, as was another young woman, ungainly with a large rear-end. She was telling them about her difficulty finding an entry-level position, due to the fact that she hadn't finished high school and couldn't 'talk posh'.

Another man, young but not handsome, oozed sexual need from every pore. And yet he wore a disparaging look on his face, as though he'd rather torture an animal than have sex, and if a woman did happen to fall into his hands, he'd treat her the same way.

Amongst them stood a woman of indeterminate age. She had hair like steel wool, and she wore a white acrylic cardigan that zipped up at the front, had holes in the back and was bunched at her waist where she wore a pouch. She spoke to no one but didn't look uncomfortable – she just hadn't found a place to park herself yet.

These people provoked such unease in him that he wondered whether they could see his misery as clearly as he saw theirs. At least he hadn't worn a puffer – he had on his dark grey coat – nor jeans and a sweatshirt – and was wearing his black wool slacks and dark grey wool sweater over a white shirt buttoned to his neck. And unlike most of the shoes in the room, his were black leather, very traditional, with shoelaces, not Velcro.

He looked at himself and saw a mousey grey man.

Mousey grey archivist, he thought.

Actually, he was too warmly dressed for the season.

Mainly grey, he thought, mostly mousey.

Not wanting to linger among these unhappy people, he went straight into the church. It was one very large room with walls clad in red-brown brick. The brick stonework created an interlacing pattern as if the walls were crocheted. He stood by the door, taking in the whole room. The ceiling was supported by metal beams from which hung small, brown lamps. The organ loft was on the opposite wall, running from one end of the room to the other, with a concrete parapet. To the right was the altar with the cross above it; painted white and made of equal lengths, it didn't look like a Christian cross; more like the Swiss flag. Something prickly was wrapped around it. To the left of the altar was a yucca plant with two arms.

The hymnals were on shelves nearby, as well as a large, folded pamphlet titled 'Church of Atonement', with a crucifixion scene in burgundy on a black background on which was printed a drawing of the church outlined in white. He took the pamphlet, sat on a stool behind the pews, and stared at the opposite wall. Between the altar, entrance and exit hung a very large painting. Early 17th century, he estimated, wondering where it may have hung originally, because the upper section of the canvas wasn't straight but curved like the vault of heaven. The painting showed Jesus on the cross surrounded by a family who were praying, their faces circled by elaborately layered white lace collars. To the left of the crucified Jesus was the father; to the right, the mother and four daughters in two rows. In the uppermost row, the mother and her two eldest daughters were dressed completely in black, except for their white lace collars, and beneath were two younger daughters dressed in the white clothes of children, with collars. The family members all had their hands pressed together as in prayer, but the hands didn't look like they belonged to their bodies. They held them like weapons, at an angle, ready for a defensive strike. They had the weapons of prayer in their hands, and their eyes were trained on the observer as if he were the one to fend off. The expression on their faces was so distrustful and unfriendly that they looked almost malicious. It was most apparent in the mother, with the two tall daughters following close behind, their mouths drawn down.

They look like me, he thought, with their white collars over black clothes and their angry faces.

Just as they looked at him, he looked up at them. And, in the same manner, he looked around the room, seeing a man from the back, in black leather trousers, black T-shirt and close-cropped hair, make his way to the organ loft. Hans' jaw was clenched so tightly it throbbed; every face muscle was tense. He busied himself with the pamphlet. To begin, he read the publishing notes (which was somewhat calming because the notes were precise). He held the third edition of the pamphlet, March 1971, and read that the first service had taken place on 11 October 1964. Presumably the reason for the pamphlet.

As soon as he opened the third fold completely (like an altar, he thought), his face cramped up again, and his jaw ached as if his teeth were being slammed into his jawbone. When he saw the famous black-and-white photos, he felt like an empty rag:

94

the bodies as thin as skeletons walking away from Bergen-Belsen, their arms wide, crucifixion-style; Carl von Ossietzky in a prison camp, his depressed face; a group of Auschwitz prisoners after their rescue. The photos related to the idea on the wall outside, left to right, that a direct line could be drawn from Golgotha to Auschwitz to Hiroshima to the early 1960s, when the Berlin Wall was erected. The reverse side of the pamphlet explained that this was the course of history. *We believe this wall is Cain's inheritance.* The church's walls were made of concrete so that *these oppressive concrete blocks reflect the violence of the other wall.* In any case completely different words might have been written on the wall. *Certainly other names might have been recorded: one need only recall the martyred, the crucified, the Inquisition, the conquest of Mexico, the Thirty Years' War, the bombings of Coventry and Dresden.* From sentence to sentence, he felt his body harden and anger rise up in him so that his blood thickened, making his heart pound harder. Now the organ began to play 'St Matthew's Passion'. The mighty organ thumped, and he heard the hymn, *FATHER FORGIVE THEM, THEY KNOW NOT WHAT THEY DO,* hammering his swollen heart. *THROUGH HIS WOUNDS, YOU ARE HEALED. Even though our path is in ruins, it is not in vain.*

Healed.

Not in vain.

Know not what they do.

All the crimes throughout history could be explained simply and satisfactorily, according to the brochure. That's why they could be listed, one after the other *we need only to remember them here.* There was a clear path from fratricide to genocide, a clear path, nothing new under the sun, all the myriad crimes of history, and those that will occur after these lines are written, with many crimes still to follow, and more to follow those, they know not what they do, now and forever, throughout the world, for eternity, amen. Man should not lose faith.

The passage ended with a prayer, *Remember us, Lord.*

It was all untrue; none of it made any sense.

Nothing would be explained, absolutely nothing, nothing whatsoever if people professed that the crimes of humanity, in essence one enormous crime, had existed from the beginning of time, and had practically been inscribed into our dear Lord's creation plan.

And throughout, the organ played around him, confusing him further. His heart, which had almost stopped moments ago, now thudded in his chest, pounding against the rhythm. His thoughts swirled around to the music and took his concentration with it. He'd heard so little of the piece, he couldn't even say what period it was from. The single, stately tones of the organ shone like a path, like a tightrope through the brick-enclosed room; the tones soaring as if they could pull him free from the muck. But the notes were always too fast to catch hold of, and he was tossed back each time, his hopes for rescue disappointed and his thoughts whirling. He would have liked to leave the church but didn't want to be rude.

The pamphlet had been published around the time of his second birthday. For so long, down so many years, people had been writing these useless words. It was depressing, too, that the pamphlet's content hadn't come from a 'state-of-the-art' archive; neither the Bureau of Past Management nor a memorial industry had existed back then, nor had any competition for the most fascinating victims, nor public-private-sponsored work-related travel to the other side of the world. Instead, only those poor Christian people fleeing in horror to prayer. The work of reconciliation and retributive justice, these were not professional matters for them, but stemmed from a deep need to prevent another crime in the future, even though they had no idea how to do that. And how could they if it was preordained in the Bible? Helpless, helpless, these prayers, and presumptuous, prideful, complacent. Hateful! And enviable. Because in the days of the church's dedication, hearts were still strong muscles that beat hard.

He watched all the other miserable people from the back pew. The woman with the blonde ponytail (not really a hairstyle, just hair pulled tight by a rubber band) sat relatively close to the handsome man, also a blond, with her arm over the pew, making a free path between her body and the object of her desire, at least as close as decency allowed. The awkward young woman sat on the other side of the man. Her arms by her sides, she kept at a distance. She'd never stood a chance.

From outside came a smell like cat urine, along with stale cold coffee and a whiff of hard-boiled egg.

Finally the music stopped. There was applause, the bald-shaved organist bowed with his hands on the gallery railing, and immediately the audience stormed out. Hans went last. People crowded onto the porch, fortifying themselves at the stingy but free buffet. Many looked glad of something to eat and may have endured the 'Long Night of the Organ' mainly for the refreshments. For example, one young man in a black faux leather jacket, with greasy hair and chapped hands, ate with such determination that he must have been truly hungry. He was ashamed and tried not to bolt his food. He stood slightly to one side, close to the little buffet table, and kept an eye on what food remained. The ladies in pastel coats, who stood in front of the word 'Golgotha', expressed their astonishment that the rolls were gone, eaten as quick as hot cakes.

Using both hands, Hans pulled his coat tight and shouldered through the crowd, anxious not to touch anyone, breathing deeply when he was out in the fresh air. He stood apart from the few smokers who were in a dark corner by the door between the church and the tower, holding his coat with both hands around his body until he felt like he was in a straitjacket and unable to move. He'd bound himself up, and because he was no longer able to move, he also knew he was there. Knew that he was he, that he existed in the world. No matter the condition of his soul and brain, his whole body held on unshakably and stubbornly, as tightly as those good Christian souls held to their belief.

Our last death-machine devoured people until it exploded. Now there is a hole in the world, a chasm where memories throng.

I slipped down among them. I'm stuck with the memories in this hole, this pit made by the world's last death-machine when it gorged itself. I endure here. To this day, I don't know what I'm waiting for.

My name is written on my forehead. I can't read it, and no one will tell me my name.

True, I'm not entirely alone – there are a few others down here with me. Sometimes we talk to each other but there's not much to say. It's hopeless. We can't help each other, we don't know what to do or say, because we are clueless.

Those who don't ask for their names have adjusted to this hole in the world. They've built a bridge over the chasm, so they won't fall in. They enjoy life.

I don't. I would be sick if I had that life. I don't even know whether or not I have such a thing – a life. If I do, it's definitely not mine.

I'd really like to know my name, but I'm stuck beside this throng of memories in the hole the last death-machine made when it devoured people. It vomited smoke and ashes, and many people, many miserable people, basted in their own fat. They burned all the better for being their own fuel. They, too, wore their names on their foreheads, but I can't read their names, they were burned. I don't know my name. They were burned.

My fuel is misery.

From above, I hear the others shout. They call down from the bridge: Come up, come and live. They call to me: You, down below - where you are, they can't tell you your name – they were all burned up.

My dearest friend, forever true, brushes dark circles around my eyes, but he won't say my name.

Wipe away those black rings from your eyes, come and live, they call again. Come to us here, live as we live, the others down below are all burned.

But I can't go to them. There's a name on my forehead I can't read. If someone came to me and spoke my name, I'd go at once with a light heart, happy to live with them – those who don't want to know their names.

An hermeneutical circle is drawn around misery with a compass. Only someone who has felt misery can cross through. And must. All others needn't cross the line, they haven't a clue. They haven't the foreboding and don't know any better; they are happy. They carry their invulnerable hearts on cake platters and don't understand us down here. Our hearts ache; we can't just expose them to air – they'd corrode and fall apart.

Come out of the hole, they call from above, everything will be all right.

But we can't climb out. For us, there's no bridge spanning the void. We can't just leave the hole; we have to work our way through. From above, the happy nameless ones spit down on us.

Darkness sheltered him. He stood stock still; if he moved, he was afraid he'd fall apart. He watched the smokers go back into the church. Soon there were no more voices, the organ began again, and he shut his eyes, but his ears would not shut, he could not shut them. He had his hands but couldn't use them; they held his coat tight around his body, keeping him together, so he would know he was alive.

When he heard steps, he forced his eyes open. Suddenly, a woman was in front of him, looking at him in alarm. She touched his arm.

'Hans, what's the matter with you?' she asked, and he recognised Graziela, the golden island in the grey sea, and because it was her, he did something he'd never done, he slung his wooden arms around her, pressing his anxious body into her broad, soft one.

She hugged him, too.

'What is it?' she said into his ear. 'What's happened?'

'I'm so glad to see you,' he said, before unclasping her. 'I couldn't stand it inside. It's so good you're here.'

Graziela left her hands on his arms, turning toward the church entrance.

'That bad? It doesn't sound that terrible.'

'It's not the organ. It's … everything. I can't go on.'

Now she looked at him more closely. She smiled. Then she stroked his head.

'You're right. After all that's happened this week, an organ concert is too much. Let's go.'

'But you need to check the acoustics.'

'I'll do it another time. Right now, I can't stand it – not the organ, the people, the church. Let's go.' She linked her arm through his and pulled him along.

'I'm parked around the corner. Come.'

Let us go then, you and I …

She wasn't wearing make-up, but her hair was brushed, and she wasn't exhausted; on the contrary, she looked fresh and well rested. Over the past few days, she had spoken of her rage, first at Joachim and, shortly after, at herself. And yet this afternoon, she said, she felt liberated, she couldn't understand how it had happened so fast. As if a stifling weight had been lifted, she felt she could breathe again for the first time in four years. It was exceptional, remarkable, and altogether wonderful.

In the car, he buckled up immediately, stuck his hands into his coat pockets and hiked the coat over his body, snugly binding it to assure himself he was alive.

'Where are we going?' asked Graziela.

'Anywhere, but not to a pub.'

'Okay, then to your place or mine.' She reasoned, 'Since I don't want to go to my place, we'll go to yours.' She turned the ignition key, and after she'd pulled out of the parking spot, said: 'I definitely need to eat something. Anything to eat at your house?'

'Yes,' he answered, his chin lifted slightly above the coat. 'Bread and wine.'

She gazed thoughtfully at the red traffic light. 'Yet where danger lies / Grows that which saves.' Also quoting Hölderlin's 'Patmos.'

'Sausage and cheese,' he said, sounding rather tired and grumpy. She didn't let herself get irritated.

A sandwich with lots of meat and very little bread, she sang from a children's poem. He interrupted:

'So how was the meeting?'

'Always the same muddle, no improvement in sight. But at least we had a chance to say how much the bureaucratic crap gets on our nerves, and that felt good. Actually it was more about hanging out together, but this shitty independent contractors' claptrap is beyond annoying. Next time I'm voting for the FDP.'

At that he was silent, and she hummed a long tone that grew into a trill of notes. She began with a few older pop songs, but didn't know the lyrics and gave up, and after more humming and trilling landed on the fourth song from Schubert's *Winterreise*, called 'Numbness' –which didn't detract from her high spirits. She hummed all five stanzas including, at the end, the piano accompaniment:

> *In vain I search the snow*
> *For traces of her steps,*
> *where, on my arm, she*
> *walked the green meadow.*
>
> *I want to kiss this ground,*
> *pierce ice and snow*
> *with my hot tears,*
> *until I see the earth.*
>
> *Where to find a flower?*
> *Where to find green grass?*
> *The flowers are dead,*
> *the grass pale.*
>
> *And am I to take no remembrance*
> *from here, then, as I go?*
> *Who when my pain is stilled*
> *shall speak to me of her?*
>
> *My heart is as dead,*
> *her image—numb within;*
> *if ever again my heart melts,*
> *even her image will go!*

It had been so long since he'd seen her this happy, and the sight was so unfamiliar that his chin crept farther towards his throat, and his head dipped into his collar. His eyes (generally he never looked up) were getting a workout, staring up at the street and traffic signs. But her singing – *If my sorrow is silent* – was slowly calming him. *Who ... shall speak to me of her?*

'Beautiful song,' he said as she sang it through again, on the next round vocalising the melody. 'And how wonderful that you came upon this particular song. It's so fitting *If ever again my heart melts, even her image will go!*' He held his head upright. 'You know what nearly killed me in the church? In the pamphlet, they expound once again on the story of Cain in order to explain Auschwitz. But not only Auschwitz: also Hiroshima and the crusades and the building of the Berlin Wall, and everything else. They always quote Cain to excuse the whole shit storm as though it was inevitable, preordained misfortune. And it makes me sick. Why not use Job as an example? No, no, it has to be Cain, "The blood of your brother cries out to me," oh, great. My own blood is crying out to me! Oh, it makes me sick, I can't tell you how sick it makes me.' As they waited at a red light, he stared out angrily at Ernst-Reuter-Platz where it was utterly peaceful.

'To speak of Job is to speak of grief,' Graziela said. 'And to speak of grief is to speak of real things, of murder and slaughter, things that really happened.' The light turned green. 'And that can't be endured.' She drove farther and repeated, 'that can't be endured.'

For a moment they were both quiet.

'That's true, too.' Then he tucked his chin back under his coat, 'Of course, you're right.' He spoke from inside the coat. Lifted his head once more: 'Of course, it can't be borne, but beating the same drum doesn't make the matter any better. It only prolongs it indefinitely. I'd prefer it if people weren't always looking at things from the outside, trying to explain the crime. Instead, speak of the suffering. I wish people would think about what it is *essentially* about. Contemplate, rather than commemorate.'

After a silent moment, Graziela began to hum, long, deep but also high tones. Calmer now, he found he could talk reasonably throughout the drive from north Charlottenburg to south Kreuzberg, travelling through the night on wide streets.

'And also what it's not essentially about,' he said. 'The terrible thing about this reasoning is that it tries to explain the crime. That's the basic fallacy. People use the Bible to explain what happened, which gives the crime meaning, as if it had to happen to prove the righteousness of their biblical worldview. And that's how the Christian religion becomes the religion of Auschwitz. As if Auschwitz weren't enough. The slaughter practically serves as an argument for God's existence. I can't bear it any longer.' He was silent. 'And it's not just Christian literature that makes this claim, in essence all the historical research is based on that same belief.'

Graziela continued humming, which was her way of concentrating.

'It's not the suffering that can't be endured,' he went on. 'What makes the research intolerable is that the pain *was* endured – by those who escaped, by those who reported it, and by those who were murdered. Really, what can't be endured is the meaninglessness of the pain, that's unbearable. All suffering. The meaninglessness of it, not the pain, that's what is unbearable. And beneath the crime's meaninglessness lies the simple realisation that everything is meaningless.'

'Hans, that sounds a little adolescent.'

'I don't care if I sound like an adolescent. That's exactly what makes adolescence terrible – that realisation. Later you forget the actual meaninglessness of life and devote yourself to its real meaning – which is to reproduce.'

'Not us.'

'We do it differently. And if not, then we're forever helping people who want to reproduce, with their reproduction.'

Graziela stopped humming and drove carefully and correctly, indicating before stopping at the light, checking her rear-view and side mirrors.

'To them the meaninglessness has a meaning,' he said, 'that's what's killing me – it's abominable. Attempting to explain the crime. Forevermore …' He broke off and was silent. He noticed she'd stopped humming, and he looked over at her. She looked at the street again, and he followed her eyes. Then he looked back at her. 'Hum a bit more, please. It's such a comfort.'

'Are you familiar with the phenomenon of acedia?' he asked after they'd eaten, having spread the entire contents of his refrigerator across his kitchen table, and, with their wine glasses still half full, they began the best part of the evening.

'Of course I'm familiar with the phenomenon,' she said cheerfully. 'I didn't only study music, lucky for you, but also theology – it was hard work – before devoting myself to flute, singing and piano. Why do you ask?'

'Tell me, why are you so happy now?'

'Because … because … hmm.' She looked at him as she thought, and her mood grew serious. 'Perhaps my time of acedia has come to an end at last,' she answered. 'Perhaps my fixation on an impossible love affair kept me from feeling any joy. Day and night, my happiness depended on Mr Joachim Humpner, engineer. I wasn't enjoying life. When I was with him, all I thought was how lucky I was, how unbelievably lucky. I'd repeat it to myself – how much better off I was than anyone else because I fulfilled this wonderful man's sexual fantasies, which I convinced myself were also mine; and if I hadn't continually repeated that mantra, I might have seen how ridiculous it was, that it wasn't happiness. I was just the fuck buddy of a henpecked husband.'

'What's happened to you?' He was completely astounded. 'You sound like a totally different person. Last week it seemed like you'd die without Joachim, and now as if you'd die if the affair went on one more day.'

She hesitated a moment.

'I think I was dead already,' she said sadly. 'The whole time it was as if I was a real person merely because someone wanted to have sex with me, and without that I'd be nothing. Really, I thought sex was the essential thing. I thought it was the only way I could be connected to other people, to humanity, only through a real, physical relationship – and that I was someone because of it. I only existed because of him.'

'You never told me that.'

'No, I never did. If I'd have told you, you might have said it wasn't true and it wasn't happiness either, and you might have convinced me, which I didn't want because I was happy. And also, I never told you, because I didn't know – I only just realised it. Over the past few days, I've figured out so much, sometimes I thought my head would burst into flames. It crackled, really, you could hear my brain working. For real! Suddenly, I understood everything. And the first thing, and this was fantastic, was that sex isn't actually the most important thing in the world, and moreover, that I am worthwhile even if no one ever wants to sleep with me. And it instantly made me so happy, I hardly knew what to do with myself, I was overjoyed. I played Beethoven all yesterday evening.'

'On the flute?'

'No, on a trampoline.'

And with that, she laughed so heartily that his heart felt warm as well, and he laughed out loud with her.

'Okay, but what's with this acedia?' she said after enough laughter. 'Why did you ask me if I knew what it was?'

Conversation came easily, in part due to the wine, but mainly due to her delight.

For the first time since he'd known her, he thought her completely beautiful and didn't trip up on her flamboyant face. She was glowing. It was as if something had been loosened in her, and not just knots that were now undone; it was as if she'd been freed of something that had imprisoned her, which he only now understood as she talked about her new insight. He couldn't have said earlier exactly what had weighed on her, at most he'd guessed, never really knew; it made him happy that she'd figured it out for herself, and what pleased him most was that her intelligence had come to light again. Sometimes he'd doubted if it was really there.

Given their happy mood, it felt strange to talk about his misery, which had disappeared for the moment.

First he had to remember how miserable he was.

'Over the past few days, I've also thought a lot,' he said finally. 'I've been thinking about my unhappiness. Why it's always with me.'

She was completely attentive, her face open and guileless; and suddenly a wall broke inside him, the wall he hid his thoughts behind. He felt as if a river flowed from him, carrying all his thoughts upon it, flowing out into the open, everything that had happened in the past few days, everything he knew or had suspected. Though his brain didn't crackle, it worked with greater precision.

His belly became very warm.

He sensed that something vital was happening, and Graziela sensed it, too, because his face was open and clear while he looked intently at her.

She smiled.

'Why doesn't your misery ever end?'

'I still don't know exactly, but, as I thought about it, I remembered the concept of acedia, which I thought might explain my misery, what it actually is. It's a hunch – an intuition. I don't know for certain. Perhaps a person can't ever know with complete certainty.'

'Acedia has been described as a state that befalls monks, a sickness that makes them lose their delight in God,' she said to help him.

First he had to get used to the new warmth and breadth in his chest and stomach. Probably an outpouring of dopamine, he thought, or a flood of some other happy hormones.

'I haven't lost joy in God,' he said at last, 'but in the management of the past. I've lost the sense that I need to do this work.

Not that I think it shouldn't be done. But I ask myself whether I have to do it. Whether I must continue, having done it now for so many years, and in these intervening years, it's no longer the essential work it once was; it's become the Shoah-Business. And that is very strange. Because for me it was never a business. Truly not. It's the opposite.' He paused a moment.

'At the same time, I'm glad that someone like me contributed to the project. But I can't any longer. I don't know what's happened, I …. I simply can't. I always thought this work was my duty, but now that obligation makes me feel like a concentration camp guard – only it's as if the guards are there to keep the memories fresh. Because we're guarding the concentration camps, too. Because we'd all be unemployed without them. What a horrible thing to say and much too simplistic.' He was silent again.

'It's strange, talking about being unhappy,' he stopped. 'Right now I'm not at all miserable.'

'So much the better,' said Graziela. 'You can describe the feeling when you aren't stuck in the throes of it.'

'Hmm.' He looked at the cheese on the table. 'Then this is the only time I've ever described it. Usually I'm stuck in it.'

'Always?'

'Yes. Day and night, summer and winter, spring and autumn.'

Graziela felt frightened. The light in her face changed to worry.

'I didn't know, but I suspected. Feared.'

She looked at the cheese, the plate, the table.

Then at him.

'Neither of us has spoken about what's most important.'

Now he smiled.

'We'd be the perfect married couple – we should get married.'

She laughed.

'Hold your horses,' she said, and they looked each other over like two old horses, beaming happily.

'Let's put this stuff away, or are you still hungry?'

'No. I'll help you.'

Graziela, dear, you have helped me.

And you have helped me, too, my dear Hans.

THEY MOVED TO HIS STUDY/LIVING ROOM. Graziela sat in the chair she always sat in when she visited, while Hans described Wolkenkraut's never varying two hundred and ninety-three versions of the account of his time in several concentration camps, and how the steady repetition had sucked the marrow from his bones.

Moreover, he told her, he believed Wolkenkraut's accidental death was a hidden suicide; and then he said he wished Mafalda Wolkenkraut had come to them before she jumped out the window – not because they'd know more about her father than they already did from those basic reports; obviously she was too young at the time of his death to add much – but they might have learned about the toll on the second generation, which the Americans had studied more than the Germans – he shook himself.

'Now I'm talking the way they do.'

'They – who? Who do you mean?'

'The Holocaust dealers and explainers,' he said. 'So dry and business-like.' And in that same moment, the lightness that had filled him over the course of the evening drained out, and he thudded back to misery, as if it were the only place for him. This is my hole, he thought instantly, I belong here, and Graziela couldn't lift him out. She tried to comfort him with practical advice: Don't be rushed. Just keep on. He'd know what to do soon. At the same time, distract yourself and don't turn down the trip to Shanghai. Don't be hurried. Look on the bright side: When would he get another chance to visit Shanghai? 'But do I want to visit Shanghai?' he said, to which she lifted her shoulders as if she could raise his spirits. But she was exhausted from her own life's tumult, particularly last week's enormous upheaval.

She only returned to the subject of Shanghai as she prepared to leave; she was going to the Baltic Sea the very next day (she'd reserved a room in Heringsdorf and needed air, she said - air!). She wanted to know exactly what type of estate had been found, and he described the schlager composer Moritz Rosenblatt, whose possessions had remained in Shanghai after his death because he'd died, tragically, only days before he was to leave for San Francisco. And after she said maybe they would need a musicologist to examine the material properly, he thought, wouldn't it be wonderful if they could work together for once?

'If you had a contract with us, you could prove that you're truly self-employed,' he said, and she smiled.

'I hadn't thought of that. Of course, that would be a nice extra benefit.'

'Come with me,' he said, possibly so softly that she didn't hear him, and then she brought the departure ceremony to a close without further ado, hugging him and humming in his ear, after which he kissed her solemnly on both cheeks.

He went right to bed but couldn't settle; there were so many things to think about that he wasn't sure which one was robbing him of his sleep. After lying awake an hour, he took a double dose of tryptophan, which led him quickly, as he wished, into a deep, dreamless sleep, first tickling both his legs, until he heard the tickle in his head. With that, he fell asleep – the whooshing sound of his brain functioning between his ears.

In the morning, he awoke in the same condition he'd found himself in the morning before, and the morning before that, and also the morning before that, and overall on all the mornings that had ever been.

He WENT STRAIGHT TO THE KITCHEN and, while he put the kettle on, recalled the last visit he'd made to Auschwitz for the opening of the International Auschwitz Committee Conference. The occasion was intended to be an encounter between survivors and young people; in attendance were various organisations, some that cared for survivors and some for juveniles in the state system. In addition, a horde of employees from official organisations, state institutions and volunteers, as well as two local Polish journalists participated; all of whom used the opportunity to network cheerfully and find new projects. As this was a unique occasion, the conference was officially sponsored; the International Auschwitz Committee had received funding from a government institution, without which the epoch-making event would not have taken place. Naturally, delegates from all divisions of the Bureau of Past Management, including the archives, wanted to attend.

He wasn't giving a lecture, but he had did have to go along with Marschner, who seized every chance for countless so-called conversations with numerous functionaries from various state and private organisations and institutions, and thus spent the whole time chatting with who-knows-who about who-knows-what. Hans, meanwhile, barely spoke to anyone except for the survivors he'd met previously, who took his hands in theirs and looked at him, always friendly, and he felt his guilt was as bottomless as their deep eyes.

At the closing ceremony, the survivors laid a wreath at the memorial where the train tracks ended at Birkenau. It was the beginning of June, somewhat warm, the land marshy, and the earth gave off a disagreeable humidity. Even before the concentration camp was built, the region was considered unpleasant; nature itself had created an uninhabitable place, a place no one would want to visit - no further event or action would have been required to keep people away. The unpleasant humidity upset his stomach, making him feel nauseated the whole time. Only those survivors who had participated as contemporary witnesses were assembled at the end of the tracks and, because they were no longer required to speak, they stood around in silence. And though there were not many people in the open, empty field, he felt he was not alone enough and quickly walked away. He couldn't bear to be near anyone in such a place.

From the memorial at the end of civilisation, where the wreath now lay, he followed the platform toward the infamous entrance gate. The best-known photo of the camp's interior had been taken from inside the gate with the tracks leading out, so no one saw them leading in; this photograph, so familiar to him, was no longer a picture, but came alive as he walked along the train platform and past the memorial, and though he couldn't stand the sight, he wasn't able to leave more quickly. Gravity was heavier in this place than anywhere else in the world. From the platform, he turned left onto the street that led through Camp Sections B II c and B II d to streets on the other side; at the second entrance gate, Section B II was directly across from the Commander's Headquarters, leading straight to the Gas Chambers and Crematoriums 5 and 4. Had led. Led.

Walking along the street between the tall, barbed wire fences, he saw endless rows of foundation walls, formerly barracks, perfectly parallel, exactly as the camp had been designed on the drawing board. As he walked along the street, it became clear to him that this was the path, the very path intended for those who were to be murdered; the street they must have walked along to Gas Chambers 4 and 5. They walked along this street between Sections B II c and B II d, but they would not have seen the foundation walls, only barracks; they must have thought that they were walking through a carefully planned city – a city builtout of horse stables, yet inhabited by human-like figures.

What am I doing? he'd asked himself as he walked along the street, already feeling sick from this damp, vaporous spot of earth; and he felt even sicker when he realised what he was doing and which way he was going. It's grotesque, he thought, I can't, I can't walk this way, not here, not of my own free will – this path leads straight from the train platform to death. Not this. I can't walk the same path as those who went to Gas Chambers and Crematoriums 4 and 5, whose bodies were burned after they walked this very street. For me there are many paths to take, I can choose another, but not this path, this one I will not walk. It is grotesque.

He couldn't turn around, there was no way he could turn away from this path, those who were made to walk this way hadn't chosen it, they'd been prodded along, not knowing what awaited them, this street took them to the gas chamber, to slaughter, to death; no way could he turn around, in those days the street was travelled once, and it went in only one direction. He couldn't turn around. The others had not been able to turn around.

In those days, electric current ran through the gateposts' porcelain sockets and along the barbed wire fence. The street led unswerving between the barbed wire fences. From here it would be impossible to change direction, there was one street and they had to walk to the very end, not so very far, in reality perhaps little more than a hundred yards. It's grotesque, he thought, what am I doing here?

At the end of the street between Section B II c and B II d, at the asphalt road, he turned right. Or rather, he didn't exactly turn, his feet more or less veered right; there, beneath his legs, his feet went on their own volition to the exit, not left toward the Gas Chambers and Crematoriums 4 and 5, which had seemed inevitable and terrifying. His body knew what to do better than he did. How to free him from this place.

To his left was an overgrown field where Camp B III had been planned but never built, to his right was the rest of the camp, Sections B II c, b and a, one after another; directly in front, he saw a large Christian cross on the Commanding Officer's Headquarters, which was now the Church of Brzezinka. During the German occupations, the village of Brzezinka was called Birkenau.

He went down this street.

He followed his feet.

At the same time he was astonished by his feet. Surprised because they knew what to do and had thought of nothing else. With his feet in his head, he continued down the camp's main street to the exit.

There he walked through the camp gates, out
onto the small country road
running alongside the fence.

And was free.

MAYBE IT BEGAN THEN, HE THOUGHT, while he warmed the pots for tea, recalling how he'd left the Auschwitz-Birkenau National Museum after that last visit, first pouring hot water in one pot and then a little into the other, this is surely the answer, tea leaves go into that pot, I only needed to trust my body, now wait a bit, it knew better than I did, until the water settles down, how to keep going, while it heats, I shouldn't have gone back, quickly pour boiling water on the leaves, I should have stayed there, on the contrary, put a saucer over the top of the pot, I should have kept going, so the tea steeps without cooling, should never have gone back to the Bureau, he stood at the kitchen counter, I should have gone somewhere else, gingerly he placed the teapot with the saucer on the thick wooden countertop, anywhere else. I've mastered this elaborate tea-making practice, he thought, to perfection, I just shouldn't have come back, no need to think twice about it, just kept going, trusted my feet. He felt the rising heat in the teapot. I fit into my life, he thought, he fitted into his life as if it were a case, he thought, as if it were an eyeglass case, I function, he functioned. My life functions. Does it?

He poured excess hot water from the kettle down the sink, at least I don't hurt myself doing simple kitchen tasks, at least he'd mastered everyday chores, every morning for a quarter of a century I've made a pot of tea, he emptied the sieve of wet tea leaves into the compost bucket, I never begin a day without a pot of tea, he took one of two large thermal glasses from the cupboard, and these days I like to drink from a thermal glass. With the glass in one hand, the pot in the other, he stepped over to the counter-height refrigerator. Putting the glass down, he poured tea from the pot into the glass, took milk from the refrigerator for the tea, and put it back, then sat at his kitchen table and took a long gulp.

It burned all the way down as if the tea were boiling hot steel, leaving his stomach glowing.

A pleasant pain.

A fire glowed in his belly, which he savoured fully with closed eyes, his right hand around the warm glass, the other in his lap.

His head hung low.

He hadn't been sitting long when Graziela called to say goodbye before she left for the Baltic. She was as happy as she'd been yesterday evening, and he was as unhappy as he'd been for the past many years.

'Hans,' she said, 'please. Simply *act* as if everything's all right. Go to the library and borrow a few travel guides.'

Graziela is leaving, he thought, and I am left behind.

'Pretend you're excited about the trip.'

And if I'm not careful she'll leave me behind forever and go off alone, or with the right man, maybe only Joseph Haydn, but without me anyway.

'Yes,' he said, 'smile for a long as it takes, until you're happy.'

'Go ahead, make fun of me. I'm only trying to cheer you up.'

And she'd be right to leave him behind – he always treated her so badly.

'I'm sorry,' he said.

'Oh, come on,' she said, 'don't feel bad. I understand, but let's not discuss this now.'

'Understood.'

'Get a few travel guides, go to the library.'

'Yes, perhaps that's the key,' he said to be polite.

After she hung up, he was thankful for her clear suggestions on how to spend the weekend. Even though he didn't want to travel, and therefore didn't want to read travel guides, he would visit a library, and not an academic one – the public library. Why shouldn't Shanghai serve as his leitmotif through the catalogue? He had to start somewhere if he wanted to do what other people did, and then, maybe, he'd begin to be like them. Smile until he became a normal person who used his free time to study a subject he'd become suddenly and fortuitously interested in, and therefore visit a place that the local government had provided for this sole purpose.

Do this like a normal person for as long as it takes to become a real, normal person.

EIGHTEEN BOOKS:

seven about pre-war German emigration to Shanghai (mainly personal accounts), the others about all manner of things, some political subjects (the war in the 1930s [Vicki Baum], the Cultural Revolution, June 1989), and some sensationalist (forced prostitution, sex change operations);

nine films:

two of which were documentaries about emigration, the others were without political content and mostly old (Orson Welles, Josef von Sternberg, Alfred Hitchcock, and Charlie Chan), but even the two more recent ones were set in that familiar mafia milieu;

one CD,

with so-called shanties, like Curd Jürgens bawling, *Sailor, sailing to Shanghai, / keep your heart tight in your hand. / Sailor, sailing to Shanghai, / stay on board and don't go on land.*

He lugged them all home.

He gave the books a cursory reading (the personal accounts) or didn't read them at all (the novels); he watched the documentaries from beginning to end on his computer, most of the other films as well (the ones with Marlene Dietrich, Rita Hayworth, and Gong Li at double-speed, and the others in total delight); he listened to the brawling song about the sailor on the CD, which took fortitude – it was awful despite the fact that it only lasted a few minutes. At least it corresponded musically and lyrically to his feelings whenever he thought about the trip.

WHEN GRAZIELA CALLED LATE SUNDAY EVENING to inform him that life was beautiful, he was inclined to agree with her.

She reported on the glorious air by the mild, rippling Baltic and told him of Usedom's many charming houses, like fin-de-siècle Berlin yet smaller overall and even more gingerbread, set upon its gentle hills. But most beautiful was the sky over the sea, she couldn't get her fill of the wide, wide sky; and he reported on the many books he'd looked at and shared tidbits from the really great films he'd seen on his laptop, and, best of all, the two early Hitchcocks found under keyword 'Shanghai', wonderful films he'd never have seen if she hadn't suggested the library! He was grateful to her. And he'd had a lovely weekend because he hadn't left his apartment since returning from the library.

They swapped their cheerful news back and forth until silence set in, and they noticed how forced and what a strain it was. The silence lasted so long it was embarrassing. Graziela inhaled deeply and then exhaled so heavily it sounded like a groan, and he thought he'd better do something quickly before all her efforts would be for naught, before her fury, her many decisions, and her trip to the Baltic would be swept away in a flood of tears.

'Shanghai as *topos* has, or has regained, the role it had in the thirties,' he began. 'It's a place where anything seems possible, where unheard-of things, in all respects, happen. In older films, this leads to eroticism, in newer ones to violence. Of course, this made good cinema – the unfamiliar incites erotic desire and fear, too – and the exotic promised to be erotic – whereas today it translates into violence.'

'Don't talk about eros, please,' said Graziela.

'Almost done – I just want to add that it's no wonder emigrants found Shanghai uncanny – all the reports bear this out. For them, it was the last refuge in every sense. The absolute end. All of them had already fled from elsewhere.'

'If man cannot flee from himself, he cannot choose his destination,' she prophesised.

'Oh, I see, you're not over it?'

She wavered a moment before she replied.

'It wouldn't happen so quickly.' She sounded remarkably neutral.

'Everything takes time,' he agreed, and she changed the topic.

'Listen,' she said.

'Yes,' he picked up the stitch.

'I've considered your suggestion that I go with you to Shanghai.'

'Yes,' he said, confirming he'd heard her.

'I don't think it's a good idea,' she said, fastening the row before beginning the next stitch.

'Somehow, I have to find myself again. I think a trip would be too exciting right now. I'm so preoccupied with myself, I wouldn't be able to focus on the city.'

So she had heard everything he'd said to her, nothing had been lost, and he could rely on her completely.

'Hmm.'

'Bad?' she said.

'No,' he said,

'it was merely an idea,' and continued,

'in all likelihood you're right.

I just thought …'

At last he knew what he wanted to say, which was: 'I need to find a way back again, too. No, not back. For the first time, I have to find myself. You once advised me to accept things as they are.'

'Yes,' she said.

'And, who knows, it might be good.'

'Yes,' she said once more, and then, at last, they really began to talk.

She told him how the Baltic had been, and he told her about the books and movies that had Shanghai in their titles, some of them farfetched and only using the city's name to attract attention. He also told her how he remembered leaving Birkenau, and that it had given him hope, and she said it sounded hopeful, it was a good sign. Then she told him about walking along the beach, how several men had noticed her, and how that had given her hope.

Good things for them both.

Even if only for the moment.

Because the next thing she told him – she tried to make it sound casual – was that Joachim had called when she got home. She'd hardly opened the door – interesting, right, as if the phone had been ringing the whole time and Joachim trying to reach her all along.

Please no, he thought.

'And?' he said.

'He wants to talk about everything.'

Of course, he thought, talk about everything.

'So his wife no longer wants a divorce?' he said.

'What?' she said. 'What makes you say that?' Unfortunately, she sounded rather jolly as she told him they were meeting the next evening. To talk everything over. She gave Joachim top marks for wanting to talk about everything – after all, there was still so much to discuss.

Great, yes, he thought, discuss it all. This one-week separation was only an episode in their story, a point in their shared history, which they would refer to later as a pause between two acts, a time of introspection. The usual.

'Whatever you want,' he said eventually, and she didn't persist with the conversation.

And with that everything was back to normal and yet completely changed. It was simply her life, that was all, her life and his life and Joachim's life and the life of Joachim's wife, and they each lived at this time and no other. This was their moment on earth and in the history of humankind, their bodies warm and their hearts beating as other hearts had and would beat; and they must do whatever they could with their time, and so forth and so on, or settle for whatever life handed them, and on and on, and find the middle between action and endurance, force and forbearance, progress and tradition, with small adjustments, first in one direction, then another, the usual, forever.

Forever.

Forever and ever and ever.

On Monday, Frau Kermer opened fire. The very day of their argument she'd sent an email telling him that Marschner 'would have time for a discussion' when he returned from the conference in Estonia on Monday. Apart from that, she had neither spoken to Hans nor acknowledged his presence

When he fetched his coat from the hall closet, she murmured in English 'same procedure than every day' behind his back, and, as if to confirm it, let a ballpoint pen flap between her fingers.

'Same procedure than every day' was wrong in three ways: incorrectly quoted, ungrammatical, and not an interrogative. So wrong it was ridiculous. With that kind of behaviour, she couldn't touch him.

Immediately, he felt at ease; her misquote and bad English were more insulting to him than any of her spiteful acts. His sense of accuracy had been insulted, but not him, not his eccentricity, not his coat tic, not his inability to be happy.

He turned to face her, his coat draped like a beloved child over his left shoulder – although, when it came to his coat, he was the child.

Same procedure as last year? he thought, which was what the drunken butler actually said in the televised British play *Dinner for One*. He watched Frau Kermer and considered whether to say this aloud, but it was unnecessary, she had already glanced away. She was two-faced, and never fought fairly. A public servant. With springing steps, he distanced himself.

Alone in the hall corridor, he stirred up a great cloud of his smiles, all that had collected up over the years, and as the many smiles flew about in the air, they kissed him up and down as lightly as butterflies, tickling his skin.

MARSCHNER WAS A GLOOMY GREY MOUNTAIN OF FLESH erupting from behind his desk. It stood at an angle in front of the window, and he sat against the light. The small desk lamp was on, striping his face with shadows top to bottom. He wore a thick, dark grey sweater without a shirt underneath, and his dark grey hair formed a ring around his head like soft, curly snakes. Deep shadows underlay his eyes. Everything about him was worry and woe. He was extraordinarily sad.

When Hans closed the door, Marschner sighed, pointing to a chair in front of his desk, and, as Hans sat, his superior watched him through his gloomy grey eyes for a long moment, his hands clasped on the table. He seemed unable to begin, as if his worry and woe, his boundless sadness could not be put into words. Combined, they were enormous – worry, woe and sadness.

Hans looked at him thoughtfully and held his gaze as if it were a simple test. And it was, since he hadn't been the cause of the worry, woe or sadness, and had merely requested a means of travel fit for a human being, along with similar accommodations in Shanghai. On his part, he felt no guilt, and believed that Marschner's dark grey appearance was hugely exaggerated. But it was part of the role his boss was playing.

If anyone should look grey and sad, it's me, thought Hans. Marschner knows nothing about true misery. Anyway, this isn't the end of the world; it's just money. And power.

And he was totally uninterested in both, a bystander watching a game of chance.

He knew, though, not to laugh. The game was easier if he concentrated on not laughing. He felt light and carefree and excited – on which colour would the ball in the roulette wheel land?

'It's difficult to say what I have to say.' At last Marschner roused himself, and Hans nearly smiled in response. These were the very words he'd anticipated.

'I'm sad to hear you're not happy with your work environment,' continued Marschner, and now Hans smiled for real, because these words were also totally expected. The smile seemed to irritate Marschner. He widened his eyes for a moment as if annoyed that Hans had thrown him off-track.

'Naturally, I understand why you want to travel in comfort, but I don't understand why you need a luxury hotel. We're not working for a private company here. I, for example ...'

That won't cut it, thought Hans.

' ... spent last week at what was once a Soviet vacation home, none of the bathrooms were renovated.' With these words, Marschner's dark grey flab changed into dark grey stone, and his dark grey eyes suddenly gleamed black.

But it had worked.

Now he'd have to change course.

He smiled at Marschner.

'And how was it by the sea?' he asked, 'I've heard Pernau is quite lovely.'

'Pärnu,' corrected Marschner.

Next strategy.

'I'm sorry, I only know the name from literature. And documents. Those not written in Estonian. Did you know David Oistrakh holidayed there for decades?'

'That's in every guidebook,' said Marschner, who'd become a glowering dark grey ball of wool. 'There's a David Oistrakh Music Festival in Pärnu.'

Now for the surprise attack.

'And what about the memorial' said Hans, 'will it proceed?'

'Nothing is settled,' said Marschner, somewhat anxiously, 'too many of the former forced labourers still alive – they would all need compensation. There's not enough money.'

Next, hit him with shame.

'So, because too many of the formerly forced labourers are surviving, a memorial to them can't be organised,' Hans pieced together. 'Hmm, and the archives?'

'Well, the archives.' Marschner heaved a sigh. 'That will be tough to arrange. Our Estonian colleagues want the remaining inventory for themselves, even though it's uncertain whether there will be a memorial. I've tried everything to persuade them, but they haven't budged. The materials would be more accessible, and so much more secure with us! Ah, you know it yourself.' Then it dawned on him again what it was he really wanted to talk about, and his dark grey pallor seemed made of pure exhaustion. He spread his hands over his face, opening all he could open – his eyes, nose, and mouth – and breathed deeply. 'You leave for Shanghai in one week. Frau Kermer tells me the flight is rather expensive because we're late to book. Let's make a deal here: You fly FinnAir economy, and we book a four-star hotel for you. How's that for a compromise?'

No contest. Too easy. And FinnAir was not expensive.

'Four stars … ' he said, hesitating, and at once Marschner jumped in to close the deal.

'Frau Kermer called the German consulate in Shanghai. Unfortunately, the guesthouse at the consulate is already booked, but they've recommended the hotel.'

'Hmm.' Hans saw that the battle was lost before it had really begun.

The agility with which Marschner had presented the answer depressed Hans. He'd been undermined by Marschner, who had simply switched their roles. Marschner assumed the part of the dark grey, miserable one, and the role of the carefree busybody fell to Hans. Marschner was a master of his craft, not intelligent but clever. He was a star on the world's stage, and Hans merely an extra.

'All right,' he said, feeling the air leak out of him. Marschner had colour in his face again. His eyes blazed with triumph, and, instead of Medusa-like snakes, the carousel swing jingled and swung around his head. He beamed at Hans, stood, and offered his hand across the table to seal his victory.

The discussion was closed, and Hans completely beaten. Without a word, he dragged himself out the door.

MANY PEOPLE WALK AROUND STOOPED OVER. Some carry the burden of history, others only their muscles, which can be heavy, too, although those carrying the weight of history can't really imagine it. The worst off, of course, are the ones shouldering the whole world.

HE'D REACHED THE BOTTOM of Wolkenkraut's bequest, only a few documents left inside the crate. He entered three more versions of the report into the archive, one of which had been made into a lithograph. Inscribed in stone. Beneath it was a child's wax crayon drawing of a house with a large red roof, over it shone a round sun with yellow rays reaching to the green earth where three figures stood: a man, a woman, and a girl in a blue dress. It was signed in awkward capital letters. Mafalda fecit.

He stared at the sheet for a long while.

Everyone's dead now, he thought. The whole family gone, everyone dead.

Terrible paper. About to crumble. Then dead, too.

It was the next to last document in the crate. He bent down deep inside for the last one, which was wrapped in thick, transparent, brownish paper stamped with a pattern. The protective paper was dog-eared, and oddly creased, having lain for so long under the weight of all the others. He opened the transparent paper and saw practically the same picture as before, except this one was without colour, made only of black lines; the child's drawing had been made into a lithograph. He saw a house with a large roof, a sun with rays reaching to the earth where the stick figures stood, a man, a woman, and a little girl, holding hands. All three had semi-circles on their faces. A single colour, black, and not signed by the daughter but by the father. Cheerful people, everyone dead. Mama, Papa, Mafalda, everyone dead. No more yellow sun, no green earth, no red roof, no blue dress. No smiling faces, only those black lines. Everyone dead.

Me too, he thought, noticing with time how dry his mouth had become. He couldn't have said how long he had been staring at the picture.

He went to the office kitchen for a glass of water. He was so thirsty he drank it down and refilled the glass. In his office, he sat some distance away from his desk where Wolkenkraut's last papers were; he didn't want to get them wet by mistake.

He sat on his chair with his arms crossed, the glass of water in one hand, sipping occasionally.

He stood by the window and looked down at the city.

He saw it stretch into the horizon. By evening the sky would beat itself bloody.

He saw the cars below: rigid, geometric shapes pulling up to the red traffic light together as if they were attached by rubber bands, and then pushing away from each other before driving off at measured intervals, making space for the next vehicles to gather. Everything is regulated, he thought, traffic lights, round-abouts, turning lanes, driving on the right, everything functions perfectly.

There weren't many people to be seen, because the road was uninviting. The few individuals not enclosed in metal were so much smaller and looked much worse off than those in cars. But they're all alive, he thought. They're all alive. Walking or push-ing the accelerator and brakes with their feet, some heavy on the clutch, all these pedals helping them get through comfortably and without much damage, on the road and in life.

And me in *my grave in the air where it's roomy to lie.*

He sat down again.

He stared for a long time at the papers on his desk.

He decided to steal them.

Setting his half-full or half-empty glass on the shelf from whence he took a cardboard portfolio, he put both documents inside; the lithograph wrapped in its old, thin protective paper;

and the child's drawing, which he wrapped in archival paper. He put the stolen goods between cardboard to stabilise them and the portfolio into his briefcase.

Then he was off.

He logged out of the archive program, where two or three hours earlier he'd typed for the two hundred and ninety-sixth, and now final time: 'Account of my time in several concentration camps, account, 1 leaf' and so on. He wrote Frau Kermer an email without any salutation, 'Buying a guidebook. Will not return today. H. F.' He shut down his computer, put on his coat, his briefcase under his arm, and walked with resolve through the dark hall, intending to ignore Frau Kermer. But she was not in her usual place. Probably on a coffee break, he thought. While he stood waiting for the lift, he feared she might return, and he didn't want to run into her. He didn't even want to take the lift knowing she'd just been in it. So he took the staircase behind the lifts. It was sunny, enclosed in glass – and a sixteen-storey smoker's retreat. A fresh-faced, newly-hired bookkeeper had once called the staircase the 'Gas Chamber' and was fired immediately.

Slowly he descended the stairs. He liked the way the old buildings below drew closer with each level, always getting larger, so that by the end, as he reached ground level, they were gigantic. And yet the doorman, saying a friendly hello, was exactly his height. This is the height of a normal person, he thought; he had become one of those tiny souls who crawl across the surface of the planet.

Left Blank for Notes

Left Blank for Notes

Left Blank for Notes

BACK HOME HE PUT DOWN HIS BRIEFCASE but didn't unpack the portfolio with the stolen papers and didn't remove his coat; instead, he left the house at once for the train to Potsdamer Platz.

He had to change at Gleisdreieck. It was his favourite underground station, large but mostly deserted. It was part of the past that existed before the one he managed, and it had been built for throngs of people. Even then, in the past before his past, people had had to quickly cross the city, and this station was always crowded – he'd seen that in old films.

Gleisdreieck was the last station before the train travelled up high on stilts over the Landwehr Canal; and then it would descend, rush deep underground, actually tunnelling through the middle of an apartment house. In the seventies, in another city district, a motorway had been built that also ran right through a residential building. It was outrageous, when he thought about it, that trains and cars should drive through people's homes, that progress should be privileged over tradition. It was, he thought, as if everyone were in a state of constant agitation, ensuring that no one would ever have peace and quiet and, perhaps, time for reflection.

He changed to the line that ran along a wide viaduct across fallow land, no longer on stilts. From the platform was a view over a long bare swathe, which was not caused by the war; it had always been there. There had once been tracks there to Anhalter Bahnhof, the old station, not destroyed in the war but demolished in the fifties.

As his train pulled in, he saw that the carriage directly in front of him was jammed with young people. Several school groups were headed into the city as part of their civic education; they were visiting the current presumed centre, located in the middle of the city between the East and West historical centres. He hesitated a moment, considered whether to get into another carriage, and then gave up, pressing into the wave of warm bodies.

Inside the carriage, shrill hilarity reigned, and he was squeezed through a crowd as thick as bread dough. These young bodies knew nothing about personal space and distance, a protective zone for each person's dignity; instead, without inhibition, they bumped and nudged against each other and him. He held on silently.

As the train carried them, they rocked as one body, and he thought again about the film *The Pawnbroker*, the film Graziela had told him about, which he'd watched again on account of her; he'd seen it once on TV, dubbed, of course. More importantly, he remembered he hadn't yet asked Graziela how she felt these days on crowded trains, if she still dwelled on the people who had been transported in cattle cars to barracks originally designed for the Wehrmacht as their horse stables. From last night's conversation, it seemed unlikely he'd have a chance to ask soon. It was more likely that they'd go on talking about her so-called love life, which he feared would continue exactly as before, never reaching a satisfying conclusion.

He was overcome with emotion that Graziela was in his life, and at the same time he grieved for her because she confused her unhappiness with Joachim for happiness; and possibly she'd confuse her new independence with misery, and then probably avoid it.

She had confused things. (And what have I confused?)

The young people all around him were bursting like new green shoots, trying desperately to be funny, making remarks meant to be funny but that weren't, at which they nonetheless issued incessant bleats of laughter, hoping their constant noise would keep their animal spirits under control. Squeezed between them and his loneliness, he longed for another person as he seldom did; it seemed to him there was nothing more important than to have a person who would talk to him, and him alone. Someone exclusively his, someone who came first for him and for whom he would also come first.

He hadn't had love, but at least he had Graziela's friendship.

In one blow, this thought forced all the air from his lungs. He was suddenly so empty he thought he might choke. Just a shell of a man.

At Potsdamer Platz, the doors opened, and the many warm bodies squeezed out of the train altogether, him, too. He had only to use his feet to climb the stairs. He did this slowly, with heavy steps.

Dutifully, he sought the bookstore on the shopping centre's first floor where, as expected, he didn't find a guidebook to Shanghai. There were only guides to the city he was in already, absolutely none for foreign cities. He knew, too, that this remarkably spacious branch of a large bookstore chain was intended for tourists, and that this particular corner was reserved for foreigners, especially English speakers. In one section, a bookcase labelled 'German History' displayed ten different books about Nazi history, as well as a thick biography of Hitler, and a book about Hitler and Stalin. Other German histories were not to be found.

Delighted to have a good excuse for a walk, he left the store by way of the shopping centre and walked toward Friedrichstrasse, where there was another giant bookstore, which he assumed would have a complete selection of travel guides.

The cinemas in Potsdamer Platz's new high-rise village were showing the latest Hollywood productions. Most of the films told implausible stories about the lives and loves of plastic people. In one way or another, the others were about the past history he managed every day. You had a choice between the 1944 assassination attempt on Hitler; a post-war love story about an illiterate female concentration camp guard and a sexually awakened male adolescent; a portrayal of Jewish partisans fighting in Belarus; or a moralistic clunker about an Auschwitz commander's son who befriends a prisoner his own age and ends up murdered with him in the gas chamber. Two were based on actual historical events; the others, in terms of history, were unadulterated fiction. Here we see, professionally and shamelessly produced, what the imagination once shockingly failed to foresee. Who needs the power of imagination nowadays? Instead, let's march straight into the gas chambers – hup-two-three – *Herzlich Willkommen!* Welcome to the horror show!

The German past is public property and has been adapted for mass audiences. At best, it is calcified, every nuance rubbed away. And no consideration is given to those who gave their accounts, witnessed the events, saw them with their own eyes, experienced and escaped them (like in *The Pawnbroker*, cf. p. 8 above); and because there were so few accounts, the history was fed into the universal storytelling-machine without a sense of loss. This history, it's true, isn't Germany's story alone – at the time the whole world was affected – but Germans were the source and have confessed without question or objection. Now the quasi-official story belongs to the world. But the story is no longer about the essential core of what occurred, which would be impossible to portray; instead, it has become the eternal struggle, as people call it, between good and evil. Now that is fabulous fodder for Hollywood! Inconceivable Evil and Absolute Good appear there, so pure and beyond discussion, a blessing. It is clear as day who to weep for and who to hate. And to top it off, the story is guaranteed to end. In Hollywood, this story sits on the same shelf as Roman history. Italians aren't bothered when Roman soldiers butcher who knows who in films, and Germans need not feel uncomfortable if a Nazi shoots a Jew. The story is merely a cipher, a code, and not about Germans. Jews and Nazis have become other words for 'good' and 'evil,' and 'the Germans' in those films aren't us. We Germans watch the films along with the rest of the world, and are vastly different from those people, having left that history behind long ago – along with the rest of the world, he thought.

It is over.

All detail and nuance have been ground out of the story of our past. Experts sift through the flour dust, but the kernel is perfect for feel-good films and not the stuff of tragedy. Instead, the guilt in that Hollywood-treated kernel is just as unadulterated as the innocence. They don't aim for the head or compassion but to beat the heart black and blue.

Black and white, good and evil, Jews and Nazis. Whack-a-Mole. This is slapstick, Punch and Judy. One might consider it tragedy but only the universal tragedy of show business. It had nothing to do with the all-encompassing actions of our forebears. Anyone still suffering over this story belongs in the past. Only incorrigible people suffer over this.

Exquisite.

Such old-fashioned people.

Like him.

The park was behind the skyscrapers. Between the memorials to Lessing and Goethe stood a new concrete pillar in fresh sand, like the many slabs of the Memorial to the Murdered Jews of Europe across the street. In fact, it looked exactly like one of those two thousand seven hundred and eleven stelae, except there was an opening cut into it. He saw a TV set in the hole, and, on the screen, in black and white, was a film of two men kissing passionately – nothing else. This memorial was in remembrance of homosexuals persecuted and murdered during the Nazi period. He looked away quickly. He knew that the men would alternate with two women for reasons of gender equity. Today was the first time he'd seen the memorial, and he wished he hadn't; their kissing nauseated him. As if he didn't have plenty of chances to see people necking and flaunting their sexuality in the park! As if he didn't have to look away all the time!

He crossed the street.

He walked straight through the enormous memorial that lay ahead like a dead city in a sinkhole. It wasn't ostentatious, he was glad of that. He had been among those against it, fearing the memorial would put an end to the story that had held him in its grip for as long as he could remember. And that was what had happened. The concrete field placed a weighty lid over the story he thought would never be finished, that he'd believed would never ever come to an end. But from its first appearance, the memorial had pleased him, precisely because the stelae nestled into the earth, barely protruding; precisely because it looked like a dead city submerged into the new city when one came from Brandenburg Gate and looked out at the skyscrapers on Potsdamer Platz. The stelae resembled long-sunken houses scoured of their individual details, only their pure form remaining. But not immersed for as long as Atlantis; their rooftops still peeked out, which was how things really were, he thought. The past rose up into the present; the two thousand seven hundred and eleven submerged concrete blocks symbolised history peeking up through what was new in the city. No one would stumble over these concrete blocks on the road to the future. The stelae field was just another interesting city site. If he stood in front, rather than walking through it, the memorial was enchanting, the open view restful for the eyes – freer here than anywhere else.

So this was it: the past was submerged in the land's core and inspired artistic projects; the past belonged to him like the ground beneath his feet.

Struggling through the field was like a little adventure; zigzagging through the dark grey concrete blocks, some were colossal, others touchingly small, each angled differently because the ground beneath some had sunk. It was like a little adventure.

Near one edge of the memorial, a pair of trees grew between the smallest stelae.

So this is what the past had become. It was not bewitching like the memorial, but burdensome, heavy and clearly imprinted onto the land and people; of course, many, many people did many, many things with it, from which they made a moral and material livelihood. The only ones still shocked by the past were those who lived with the history, who knew what had actually happened, the real events. These atrocities were not fit for the entertainment industry and could not be assimilated.

At the back of the memorial, a few small streets were blocked off where stairs ascended to street level. These were the emergency exits for the memorial's information centre. The Bureau's archive had supplied the materials for the centre. He and the curator had chosen all the content together, so he knew what was there. This assignment had helped his archive to thrive in the first place. Marschner had cleverly demanded as much money as possible from the government, had used it to upgrade and complete the 'state-of-the-art' archive he was so proud of, and, with that, ensured it would never close. There was too much money sunk in it.

The street behind the memorial was named after the economist Cora Berliner, who had been deported to Minsk in 1942 and then presumably murdered in the nearby extermination camp, Maly Trostenets. The cross street was named after the philosopher Hannah Arendt, who had emigrated in 1933, and the extended street named after the poet Gertrud Kolmar, a forced labourer taken by the SS during 1943's Operation Factory, to Auschwitz, where she died. On Cora-Berliner-Strasse stood a one-storey building with tourist shops selling coffee, sweets, sausages, beer, postcards and knick-knacks. The row of stores, with sunlit, white-painted clapboard and wooden blinds, looked as elegant and peaceful as a French beach promenade.

He walked past, turned left onto Wilhelmstrasse, right onto Unter den Linden and continued to Friedrichstrasse.

In the large bookstore, the travel section on the third floor had a hundred and thirty yards of shelves dedicated to travel, as well as thirty-two feet of display tables for yet more guidebooks. Such abundance made it obvious that the store was meant for locals, whose favourite diversion was travel, and the reason for that was Germany itself – the place they wanted to run away from as often as possible. On his way through this huge store, he'd seen nothing in any form to remind him of the past he managed. Just imagine you are already travelling, he thought, you are elsewhere, nowhere near the centre of the Reich's former capital city.

He had a choice between nine guidebooks for Shanghai, six in German, two in English, and one in both English and German. In addition, there was an audio guide. One by one, he held each of the nine books, but was too weak to open any of them. So he went back down the three flights of stairs and left this bookshop, too, without buying anything. His feet carried him to the underpass of the Friedrichstrasse train station, where he knew there was a kebab shop. He bought a kebab and went outside to eat at a small counter.

The Admiralspalast, the large theatre diagonally across from him, was decorated with strange flags. Long red banners with white circles containing something black, and many black-white-and-red pennants, looking from afar just like the banners and pennants he knew very well from the past he managed. When he was finished eating, he returned his plate and crossed over to the Admiralspalast. The banners and pennants had thick pretzels printed on them instead of swastikas; he saw that some even had currywurst on them. Historically speaking, this was inaccurate. Currywurst had been invented only after the war. The flags were advertising *The Producers*, a new musical based on the film (1968, writer and director: Mel Brooks) about the production of a musical titled *Springtime for Hitler*. The title song had this refrain:

> *Springtime*
> *for Hitler*
> *and Germany ...*
> *Winter*
> *for Poland and France.*

The Admiralspalast, which had opened in 1910, had been renovated specifically as a theatre for operettas during the history he managed.

A 'Führer's box' had been built at that time.

Hitler was fond of operettas, his favourite being *The Merry Widow*, by Franz Lehár.

The operetta was performed here with Johannes Heesters in the role of Count Danilo.

Count Danilo enters the stage with the song 'I'm off to Chez Maxim's ...'

Dmitri Shostakovich used this song's melody in the first movement of his Symphony No. 7; it is repeated eleven times as the music becomes more and more violent, until it is nearly unbearable.

Shostakovich wrote his Symphony No. 7 during the Nazi siege of Leningrad that lasted from 8 September 1941 until 27 January 1944.

And so on.

Neither Shostakovich nor Franz Lehár called out to his heart, only *Springtime for Hitler*.

Humming it to himself, he went cheerfully back to the station.

The song put him in such a good mood that he went through the underpass to the ice cream shop on the other side.

There he bought himself a cup with three scoops, chocolate, vanilla and raspberry: black, white and red. Instead of a pretzel, the salesman put a wafer on top.

He hummed the same tune over and over – the song had such a catchy melody.

Auschwitz lives in every song,
every flower, every tree.
Auschwitz lives in every song,
every German, including me

Fiderallala, fiderallala, fideralla lala la.

To HOLD A CUP OF ICE CREAM and feel happy – all at once – was overwhelming, so he was glad of the chairs a few steps away near a self-service café in a 'plaza,' a development on the site where the International Trade Centre had been before the GDR perished.

There he sat right down,
crossed his legs with a moan,
watched the folks go round
and ate his ice cream alone.
And *tandaradei,*
he thought, as the crowd strolled by,
and *fiderallala,*
hooray, hoorah,
and thought some more, till he was happy, for
the harder he thought the sooner
he'd come to the end, and it was better
not to brood too much longer.

Black-white-and-red, the ice cream melted in the cup. He set it on a small table nearby because he needed both hands to hold himself together.

It seemed as if his stomach was about to explode; and he didn't know whether he would be terribly sick or horribly depressed.

It turned out to be laughter.

He held his belly and laughed, laughed and laughed.

Insane laughter, naturally, but it was laughter. He'd suddenly gone crazy, of course – what else could he do? It was only natural he'd gone crazy.

If the past he managed every day hadn't resulted in the death of fifty million or more people, he might have laughed so much sooner.

Ten minutes after the fall of the GDR, people began laughing. Just a tiny fraction of the death toll, and one could laugh much sooner.

He had to laugh, but it gave him no pleasure. Nor could he stop. The laughter was laughing at him.

Tragedy, farce, goose step, these odd words flew through his head, but they had no meaning any more, they were just groups of letters. Schultz, steel helmet, Waffen SS, *to join the whirling stream*; and it was a great relief when something inside began to howl, the tears washing all the words out – concentration camp, sonderkommando, Third Reich – this weeping and sobbing was as insane as his laughter. He hugged himself with both arms, held on tight and rocked gently.

That definitely helped.

Very soon, his sobbing stopped, and he became quiet.

He found a tissue in his coat pocket, blew his nose loudly, and then sat quiet and empty, staring at the ground beneath his feet.

All quiet.

All empty.

No words in his head, no feeling in his body – as though he didn't exist.

This was like happiness to him.

The ice cream in the cup had become a thick soup of indefinite colours – brownish, greyish, reddish. Soggy, the nibbled wafer floated inside.

It was over.

At least for now.

For now, it was past.

THE HOOKED CROSSROADS.
  The Meat Hook.
  The Hook and Eye.
  Velcro.

Referenced Texts

Every attempt was made to insert citations of translated poetry and song into the text whenever they were referenced. Those that could not be included are listed below. Any translations not cited below are my own.

p. 15 The author is riffing on and referencing Friedrich Hölderlin's diary notes and his poem, 'Half a Life.' Translated by Richard Seiburth, the stanza ends, 'And drunk with kisses / You dip your heads / In the sobering holy water.'

p. 67 'Children's Hymn', Bertolt Brecht, 1950; translated by Michael Geisler.

p. 86 *Vorentwürfe von Moderne. Antike Melancholie und die Acedia des Mittelaters*. Berlin, New York: Walter de Gruter: 1996. *Early Sketches of Modernity*, Michael Theunissen. The selected text was translated by Sophie Duvernoy.

p. 101 From 'Patmos,' *Hymns and Fragments*. Friedrich Hölderlin, translated by Richard Sieburth. Princeton University Press: 1985.

p. 102 *Die Winterreise* (Numbness), Franz Schubert. *The Fischer-Dieskau Book of Lieder*, chosen and introduced by Dietrich Fischer-Dieskau. English translations by George Bird and Richard Stokes. Amadeus Press/Limelight Editions, NY: 1995.

p. 136 'Death Fugue,' Paul Celan, translated by Jerome Rothenberg.

Translator's Note

I met Iris Hanika on a cold February day in New York City in 2016. We took a walk along the East River to Harlem and back down the north end of Central Park, talking without a pause. Not long after, she gave me a copy of her fifth novel, *Das Eigentliche*. The opening chapter read like a lyric poem, a cry from the heart, and it drew me in immediately. Iris Hanika's novel is about the psychic cost and legacy of collective guilt explored through the experience of Hans Frambach, a contemporary, middle-aged Berliner undergoing a life crisis.

An archivist, Hans works at the prestigious 'Bureau of Past Management,' whose mission is to memorialise the victims of the Holocaust. The German title of *The Bureau of Past Management* is philosophical in nature. *Das Eigentliche* could be translated into English as 'the quiddity,' 'the essence,' 'the essential' or, perhaps, 'the real thing,' but that is too colloquial. In German, conceptual adjectives are more easily turned into nouns than in English. As a result, *Das Eigentliche* sounds interestingly abstract in German, and perhaps comes across as pretentious in English. For me, the book's central question was not, 'what does it mean to be German?' but, instead, 'how do we understand the past, and what is the purpose of collective, historic guilt?' I looked for a title that would lead the reader to consider these issues, and, at the same time, reflect Hanika's irony and sympathy.

The Bureau of Past Management is the brilliant central fictional device of the novel. I have carried the institution's title into English with the irony that is implicit in the German, but Hanika's *Vergangenheitsbeswirtschaftung* is also a pun. The actual German word is *Vergangenheitsbewältigung*, denoting a process, well-known to every German, which means 'coming to terms with the disturbing events of the past.' Translating a pun is nearly impossible, and explaining a pun is as deadly as explaining any other joke, but it's useful to know that the term describes an undertaking that began after the Second World War and continues still (provoking many complicated political arguments and responses). *Vergangenheitsbewältigung* is a portmanteau, made up of *Vergangenheit*, meaning the 'past' or 'history,' and *Bewältigung*, meaning 'coming to terms with.' Hanika substitutes *Bewältigung* with *Bewirtschaftung*, and creates a pun, *Vergangenheitsbewirtschaftung*, which means the 'cultivation' or 'management' of the past. In reality, of course, there is no government office nor institution like the Bureau of Past Management that 'manages' those disturbing events.

One of the surprising ways the novel handles these events is through citations, allusions, cultural references, and quotations, many in their original languages. Hanika's novel brims with references in every genre: poetry, popular songs, opera, film, politics, philosophy, arcane facts about Berlin, and more. An early delight of mine was simply identifying them—a children's song? Bertholt Brecht? Celan? Punk rock? Hölderlin? The protagonist, Hans, is not only an archivist but also a polymath, an obsessive collector of trivia as well as facts. Some of his internal monologues mirror that knowledge reservoir in seemingly endless German sentences. Although it was important to me to keep a semblance of his overflowing sentences, I have changed the structure to reflect English syntax, and used dashes to indicate his breathlessness. His constant documentation, as well as his profession itself, is a somewhat ironic allusion to the Nazis' well-known penchant for extensive record-keeping. While I did not want to footnote the novel, which I felt would weigh it down (among other issues), I have lightly glossed some references in-text to make their origins more available to an anglophone reader. These citations, allusions, and references add important layers of texture to the novel, and contribute to our sense that the work is an experimental collage of story, history, and culture.

The sometimes painful (and sometimes hilarious) reiteration of distress and misery that characterize Hans served as an important anchor for me as a translator. Hanika portrays how history and Hans' archival work have drained him as he works in the 'vineyards of memory'. We see him archive the documents of a survivor named Wolkenkraut and the repetitious accounts of imprisonment in concentration camps. Conveying Hans' despair over National Socialism, the Nazi 'crime' as he puts it, alongside his personal misery was a challenge. I was very aware of how careful Hanika was to reveal his personal crisis through subtext and metaphor, and to not compare it to those who suffered as victims of the Holocaust. I tried to translate Hans' misery through word choice and sentence structure. In an early chapter, for example, Hans sees that 'Wolkenkraut had never dated these reports, so it was impossible to establish whether he would have broken the lines more sharply over time or found his way to a continuous text'. Hans, by analogy, is also lost, possibly even broken; 'found his way' seems to me to reflect Hans' intense need for a coherent narrative – a sense of self.

Although Hanika's novel is set in contemporary Germany, it addresses issues of memory and collective guilt that remain relevant in much of the world as we continue to grapple with the legacy of systemic racism, colonialism, intolerance, and injustice. For change to occur, history cannot simply reside in monuments and archives. As James Baldwin wrote in his 1962 essay, 'A Letter to My Nephew': 'This is the crime of which I accuse my country and my countrymen and for which neither I nor time nor history will ever forgive them, that they have destroyed and are destroying hundreds of thousands of lives and do not know it and do not want to know it.' The effort to remember and memorialize should not lead to comfortable passivity; it must inspire meaningful change.

I want to thank the editors at *Asymptote* and *Epiphany Literary Review* for publishing excerpts of this translation. I am very grateful to the Bread Loaf Translators Conference community, and to the Deutsche Akademie Rom Villa Massimo for inviting me to stay there to work together with Ms. Hanika. Huge thanks to the many generous writers and translators and native German speakers who offered advice as I worked on this translation. Last, but not least, to Iris Hanika, my deepest thanks for her trust.